MW00508495

I'M A FIGHTER

Paul Jensen

Copyright © 2022 by Paul Jensen

All rights reserved.

No portion of this book may be reproduced in any form without written permission from the publisher or author, except as permitted by U.S. copyright law.

Contents

Chapter 1

Scene 1

Lena

Eight words. That's all it takes to ruin my day.

"LaFontaine, I have a special assignment for you."

I recognize the voice without looking up from my desk. It's my prick of a boss, Adrian, and anything he's terming a "special assignment" will inevitably be a nightmare. That's all I get these days. The unfixable cases. The spoiled, self-entitled sports stars who screw up so badly, no one else wants them.

God, one massive win and I become the go-to public relations girl for the biggest jerks-with-abs in Vegas. Why can't I, just once, get a client who's a marginalized feminist with a cause? Sighing, I raise my head and meet Adrian's beady little eyes. This douchebag has my career in his hands, and he knows it.

"What's the case?"

His thin lips curl in a self-satisfied smile. It doesn't escape my notice that he's yet to close the door, which makes me wonder if he's keeping it open as an escape route.

"Jase Rawlins."

Oh. Hell. No.

"Nuh-uh," I say. "No freaking way."

Jase "The Wrangler" Rawlins is one of the bad boys of MMA. I don't even have to ask why he needs our services. Anyone who pays attention to the sports industry knows his ex-girlfriend has come forward with allegations of domestic abuse. I've seen photos of her bruised cheek and read the story in popular magazines. The guy is violent. But I suppose I shouldn't expect any different from a cage fighter.

I know the type. I've dated the type.

"There's no way I'm working with that asshole. Absolutely not. Find someone else. I'm not aiding and abetting a jackass who thinks he can get away with hitting women."

The door opens wider, and Jase Rawlins himself steps into my small, airy office, his gaze immediately drawn to the view out the window, which looks over the business district. I know him on sight, and I'm not even sorry he overheard my comment. He deserves all the condemnation he gets, and more. Fuck him.

Adrian's brows draw together, as if he didn't expect me to argue. "Everything is organized, Lena. The papers are signed. It's a done deal."

My teeth scrape together loud enough I'm surprised no one else hears them. I meet Jase's eyes, and a jolt runs through me. They're a strange color. Dark gray, or maybe green, it's hard to tell, and fringed with the thickest lashes I've ever seen. Pretty eyes. Out of place on a man known for choking his opponents into submission. He has high, arrogant cheekbones and plush lips, although the upper one is marred by a thin scar.

This is a face a woman could study forever—if she wasn't too caught up in his body. Because holy shit, he has a body. Broad shoulders, tapered hips, and strong legs with muscled calves showing beneath his shorts. Unfortunately, however panty-meltingly hot he is, he's also a brute, and I'm done with men like him. If I have anything to say about it, I'm not touching another MMA superstar—not with a ten-foot pole.

Time to shut this shit down.

"I'm not working with you," I tell him, and watch for a change in his expression, but his only reaction is a quick flick of his eyes to the right, where a man in an expensive suit has followed him into my office. "This is not a happening thing." I aim this comment at the suit, and he glowers. I don't care. There are some jobs even I won't take, and Adrian wants me to cross a moral line I'm not prepared to.

"Lena," Adrian says in a cautioning tone. "Hold on a moment."

Crossing my arms over my chest, I stare at him, wondering how far he's prepared to push. Considering Jase Rawlins is worth seven or eight figures, I'd hazard a guess that dollar signs are flashing in Adrian's eyes. Too bad. I don't operate that way. Money isn't my driver, and he knows it. So what approach will he take?

Chapter 2

Scene 2

J ase

Sometimes, I wish it was legal to put someone in a chokehold outside of the cage. Like this uppity image specialist, for instance. Yeah, she may look like a schoolboy's wet dream in an ass-hugging pencil skirt and V-necked blouse, but it's obvious from the second she opens her mouth that she's already judged me and found me wanting. Nothing I'm not used to, but it still stings.

Maybe it's the fact my dick has some really great ideas about what he'd like to do with those gorgeous red lips, which are currently set in a sulky pout, or maybe it's her instant dismissal, but I want to rile her. To ruffle up her silky feathers and find out just how mouthy she can get.

I step forward before her boss can intervene, and raise a hand. As expected, everyone falls silent, which only seems to piss the redhead off more. Fuck, we haven't even gotten as far as exchanging names before she's mentally convicted me. That's the shitty part of being in the public spotlight. Everyone thinks they know me. They believe every stupid lie anyone tells.

Well, guess what? This girl doesn't know a goddamn thing.

"Calm down, cutie pie." I love it when her eyes chill to an icy blue, silently threatening to cut my balls off. Yeah, I knew she'd hate the pet name. Considering what she thinks of me, I don't give a crap. "Turns out, I don't want to work with you either." I raise a brow at Nick, my manager, and ask, "Is this really the best you could do?"

The redhead gasps, and I want to check whether she's crossed her arms tighter over her chest, plumping her little tits up, but I resist the urge to look.

"We can go somewhere else," Nick says. "I was told these guys are the best for miracles, but I'm sure we can find someone else just as good."

"Now, wait a minute," the stuffed shirt interjects. I wasn't listening when he introduced himself so I didn't catch his name. "Lena is the best there is. You won't find anyone else."

Finally, I succumb to the desire to glance at her and see how she's taking this. I catch the tail end of an eye-roll, and it makes me soften toward her a little. She's not drinking up the flattery the way some might.

Lena. I try her name out. It suits her. Pretty, bordering on pretentious but not overstepping the mark.

"Whatever puppy dog stunts Lena"—I emphasize her name now that I know it—"wants to pull, they aren't going to do jack." I address Nick. "I still don't get why we're here. Give it a couple of days; Erin will decide she doesn't want to act on her threats, and the hubbub will die down."

Lena's face twists into a sneer. "Die down?" she demands. "The only way this shit-nado is dying down is if someone gets proactive about putting out your fires, and fast. Also, have a little respect for your girlfriend."

"Ex-girlfriend."

"Whatever." She says it like the "ex" part doesn't matter. As if Erin and I didn't break up more than two months ago now. "She's not some problem that will disappear if you ignore her. Domestic violence is a serious crime, and you can't just hand-wave it away." Her nose crinkles like she smells something bad. "It disgusts me that you're callous enough to think otherwise."

Callous? Me?

I count to five in my head and remind myself she doesn't know me. Her perception of me is based on what she's seen in the news, and I have to admit, it's damning. It also isn't true, but I don't bother saying that because this woman isn't going to believe me. Stuffing my hands in my pockets, I decide the best way to deal with her is to call her bluff.

"Okay, so you say the problem isn't going away on its own. What did you have in mind to fix it?"

"I... I..." She flounders, and I can't stop the smile that tugs at my lips. She's all bluster and no bite.

"That's what I thought." I turn to leave, but her smarmy boss lays a hand on my arm. When I stare at it, he snaps it back like he's been stung, his cheeks going pale. This guy is even worse than Lena. At least she has the balls to say what she thinks to my face. He's the type who'll pretend to be on my side, but all the while he's secretly fucking terrified of me.

"Wait, wait, wait," he says. "Give me two minutes to speak to Lena in private and talk her around. I promise you won't regret it."

Lena looks like she wants to bash him over the head with a paperweight, and I don't blame her. He's a condescending little shit. "Adrian—" she says.

"My office." He snaps his fingers, like he's ordering a dog to heel. "Now."

They leave, her trailing behind, practically dragging her feet, and Nick gives a low laugh. "Good old Jase. Always charming the ladies."

I jerk a thumb at the door. "Can we go? I've had enough of this."

He sighs, his expression regretful. "I wish we could, but what she said is true. Whether you want to believe it or not, this situation has the potential to derail your career."

"How can it, when I have the championship bout so soon? I'll blow Karson out of the water, and everything will be fine."

Nick ums and ahs. "That's if you don't get arrested before the fight."

"Pfft." I shake my head. "Not gonna happen. Erin is full of hot air."

"She also has a taste for the spotlight, and she'll keep spouting this bullshit as long as the cameras are rolling." Damn, he's right, and he must sense he has the winning hand because he powers on. "Not to mention, you promised Seth you'd take this seriously and do whatever you could not to tarnish the reputation of Crown MMA gym."

Ouch. Low blow. Nick knows I'd go to war for Seth if he asked. My trainer gave me everything. He had faith in me, took a chance on me, and he had no way of knowing I'd pan out to be a good investment. I was just a kid from a poor neighborhood with a mother of a chip on my shoulder and a willingness to shed blood to escape.

"Fine," I concede, not surprising either of us. "I'll hear them out."

But I have a bad feeling about this, and my gut doesn't often lie to me.

Chapter 3

Scene 3

L ena
Have I mentioned I'm sick of Adrian's power plays? He's only one rung above me at our firm, but he milks it for all it's worth. Like taking me aside for a word in private. What a douchey move. Does he think he can intimidate me into doing what he wants? If so, he's sorely mistaken. I'm not the kind of person who responds well to threats.

Adrian closes his office door behind us and crosses to sit at his desk, as if to emphasize the difference in our positions. While my office is nice enough, his is large and lavish, with expensive furnishings he probably bought to make himself seem more important. As big as Jase Rawlins's ego is, Adrian could equal him. Maybe. I recall how Jase appraised me, and the way my body responded, liking his attention. Craving it. Shit, I have bad taste in men.

"I don't want to represent him," I tell Adrian, as if he hasn't already figured this out. "He's a dirtbag."

"He hasn't been charged," Adrian reminds me, scribbling on a piece of card, as though he doesn't care about me in the slightest. I know better. He doesn't want to let on how critical this job is.

I snort. "As if there's any doubt." These guys are always guilty of the things they're accused of. Whether they're held accountable in a court of law is another story. By the time I'm finished with them, they usually walk away free and clear, with all the public adoration their heart desires.

Have I mentioned I hate my job?

Well, not my job, per se, but the clients Adrian assigns to me. I want better people. Ones who are trying to make a difference. Good people in bad circumstances. But apparently, that's not where my strengths lie. I've had this discussion with him more times than I can count.

Finally, he looks up. "Tell you what, Lena, you dig Jase out of this hole and you can choose who you take on next. What do you say?"

I gape, my mouth opening and closing like a goldfish before I snap it shut. He must be lying. He'd never let me do that... would he? This gig is clearly important to him. Maybe important enough to sacrifice his leverage over me.

"Are you serious?"

"One hundred percent."

I'm tempted. God, it's all I've been asking for since I started here. But will Adrian keep his word? Does it even matter? We both know he can order me to work with Jase Rawlins and fire me if I refuse.

My jaw tightens. "I'm going to hold you to that."

"Good." He twists his pen, and light glints off gold. "Then go back and make things better with him. I expect to hear a report later today."

"You're not coming?"

He smirks. "I trust you can handle it, but you might have some ground to make up."

Tell me about it.

Departing his office, I trek down the hall. A moment later, I'm standing in front of the reprehensible Jase Rawlins, about to eat crow.

"I'll work with you," I tell him.

A slow, cocky smile splits his face, and he raises a broad shoulder, then drops it. "I'm having second thoughts."

"You... what?" He's playing with me. He must be. If he didn't want to work with me, he'd have left by now.

His expression is pure smugness. He's enjoying this. "I prefer my employees to be more excited to work for me."

"Jase..." Nick cautions.

Jase doesn't respond. I grit my teeth and don't point out that I'm neither his employee, nor a prospective employee. He's a prospective client. I'm not his subordinate in any way, shape or form, nor will I ever be. But Jase is the ticket to the job of my heart, and if he wants me to kneel and worship at his altar, so be it.

I imbue my next words with as much sincerity as I can muster. "You're mistaken."

He smiles at me like an eager kid who just pulled a prank and can't wait to see what happens next.

"There's nothing I'd like better than to work with you." I can't bring myself to say "work for you." I just can't. "Will you give me a chance?"

Chapter 4

Scene 4

Jase

Oh, she's hating this situation, and her sour expression makes my day. Lena thinks she's better than me, and she's dying inside with every word she says. I'm sure it makes me a bad person to take joy from her pain, but at this point I've got to get my thrills wherever I can. Everything else about today has been shitty.

"I'll think about it," I reply, wondering how far I can push before she snaps. There's fire beneath that frosty exterior, and I want a front row seat when it ignites. Nick shoots me a look. Killjoy. "Okay. Partners." I stick my hand out, and she surprises me by taking it. I half expect her to spit on me. As we touch, my nerves zing, and a muscle spasm shoots from my hand to my shoulder. Flinching, I let her go, and scowl when she wipes her hand primly on her skirt.

Jesus, what just happened? Is something wrong with my arm? I can't afford to be in less than peak physical condition the week before a fight. I shake it, but everything feels fine now and when I tense the muscles one by one and wriggle my fingers, they seem to be in working order.

"Why don't you have a seat?" Lena asks, maintaining a solid three feet of distance between us as she heads for her desk. A sweet scent like vanilla ice cream wafts in her wake, and I can't help dragging it into my lungs to savor. She gestures to the chair directly across from her. "Sit."

I sit. Nick stays where he is.

"Good boy."

Great, now she's treating me like a dog. At least dogs get pats. I doubt I can convince her to pet me. Worth a shot though. I loll my tongue out and pant.

She is not amused. "Grow up, Rawlins."

"I'm plenty grown up, cutie pie." If she can't see that the body behind my clothes is all man, that's her loss. Besides, I've got to be older than her. The creamy, unmarred skin of her forehead gives her away. Of course, my perception could be skewed because most of the faces I see have taken some hard knocks.

She sighs and glances at the ceiling as though begging the universe for patience. "Why don't you share your side of the story?"

"Nuh-uh." I shake my head. "Not gonna happen."

She stacks her hands one on top of the other and leans forward. "Why not?"

Because she won't listen. They never listen. Once a person's mind is made up, there's little I can do to change it, and she already believes I'm the bad guy. It's evident in every impatient tap of her foot, and the slight narrowing of her eyes. She doesn't want to know the truth, she just wants me to feed her a line of bullshit she can sell to the media. An excuse. But excuses are for the guilty.

I don't tell her any of this though. What's the point? Instead, I shrug. "Can't be bothered."

Her hands twitch, fingers curling as though she's imagining wrapping them around my throat. The image is so ludicrous I have to laugh.

"You think this is funny?" she asks.

"Come on, it is a little." This only seems to make her madder. "You should try it," I suggest. "Take a shot at me. See how much damage you can do." I'm goading her, but I know she won't respond.

Predictably, she notches up the ice factor. "I'm a professional, Mr. Rawlins, and for me to do my job, I need you to tell me the truth."

"Now I'm 'mister'?"

Cue eye-roll of epic proportions. I'm growing worried she might actually invert her eyeballs. That would be a shame. They're pretty. Nick clears his throat, loudly and vigorously.

I swivel to face him. "You all right, there?"

He sighs. "Remember why you're here, Jase."

Seth.

"Fine." Turning back to Lena, I try to be reasonable, for Seth's sake. "I know you want to do your job, Lena, but I'm not the kind of guy to gossip or share rumors. To be honest with you, I don't see the point in any PR stunts because Erin will find someone else to harass eventually. She's just enjoying her five minutes of fame, and as long as I play it cool, it will die off. If I try to fight back, it will just confirm the rumors. I'd be better off training for my big fight against Karson Hayes next Friday."

She cringes when I say Karson Hayes's name. Or is that my imagination? I study her, looking for a hint of discomfort but she's cool as a cucumber at a cocktail party.

"I've been trying to tell you, Jase." Her face scrunches with something like pity. "This isn't going to go away like you think it is."

"You don't know that." She doesn't know Erin the way I do.

"I'll be the first to admit, I don't know everything," she begins, and when I laugh, she smiles in response. A cascade of tremors stir in my belly. Strange. I poke one of my abs but it feels firm, the same as usual.

"But," she continues, "this is my field of expertise. Yours is MMA; mine is public perception. I wouldn't get in a cage and expect to have any outcome other than getting clobbered. If you try to manage this on your own, you'll be the one taking a clobbering, if you get my meaning. Shall we each agree to stick to what we know?"

It's a good analogy, but unfortunately now I'm picturing elegant Lena in an octagon, wearing nothing but shorts, a sports bra, and a snarl. She'd be fierce. She's totally underestimating her mean streak.

"So, what you're saying is, me ignoring this would be equivalent to you getting in the ring with Killer Karson?"

This time, she doesn't cringe when I mention the other fighter's name, but something flickers behind her eyes. "Essentially, yes."

I whistle. "Have you seen him fight? I've been in the ring with him. The guy is nasty, but this time, I'm going to make him my bitch."

Her palms slam onto the table, side by side. "I can't work with you if you're going to be like this."

The jab strikes true. "Fine by me."

She groans, and fuck, I want to hear her makethat noise in another setting. One with a bed and significantly fewer clothes. "You.Are. Impossible."

Chapter 5

Scene 5

Lena

I underestimated Jase Rawlins when he came through my door this morning. I knew he was violent, and within a few seconds, I knew his ego could fill a room, but I ranked him lower on the annoyance scale than the dickheads I usually work with. Now I see I was wrong. Not only is he dangerous, he's also a first class pain in my ass.

Is he hamming it up in front of his manager because he doesn't want to admit he's worried, or is he actually this much of a jerk? If I get him alone, maybe he'll tone it down. It's worth a try.

"Why don't you and I talk in a private meeting room?" I suggest.

It's instantly obvious I've miscalculated. Jase looks me up and down, eyes blazing hot, and I fidget beneath his scrutiny. It's like the guy has x-ray vision and can see under my clothes. He practically smolders.

Off limits, I remind myself. He's a bully and a client. It doesn't get much more wrong for me than that.

His lips hitch up. "If you think being alone together will make us productive, then I'm down for that."

Regret filters through me, but I can't back out, so I nod, select a pen and notebook from my desk, and mask my jitters as I take him to the nearest interview room, leaving his manager behind. It's smaller than my office, and has no windows, only a round table and two chairs. When I sit, my back is to one wall and when Jase slides into the chair opposite, the door can barely close past his shoulder.

He's watching me curiously, as though I'm an exhibit at a science museum, and his fingers drum on the table. They're sturdy, to match his massive palms. Good for punching people—or choking them, I suppose. As I watch him, his lips part and his pupils expand, swallowing the light. This close, I can tell his irises are more gray than green, the color of slate.

He chuckles, the sound dark and lazy. "Are we going to start, or do you just plan to stare at me?"

My cheeks flame. This morning may be the least professional I've behaved in my life. Something about him provokes me. Perhaps it's his attitude. Perhaps it's the similarities to my ex. Whatever the case, I need to tread carefully so I open my notebook to the front page, where I keep my standard list of questions, and dive right in.

"What do you do with your spare time?"

"Eat and sleep."

I record his unhelpful answer and skip to the next question. "Do you drink or do drugs often?"

"No."

If I didn't know how disciplined fighters need to be during a training camp, I'd be dubious. Jase Rawlins looks like the type to party hard. "Is there anything in particular I should know that you haven't told me?"

He shrugs. We both know the answer to that. He hasn't told me a goddamn thing.

I swallow my irritation. "Are there any other women likely to be pissed off with you?"

"No." He stifles a yawn, as though I'm boring him. "Are we nearly done?"

I glance at my notepad. There are another twenty questions to go, and if he continues in the same vein, I'm going to get very little useful information out of him. Still, something is better than nothing.

"No." I circle the previous question, deciding to do my own research on the matter. If he's hit one woman, chances are he's hit another. "Do you donate to charity?"

"Yes."

Color me surprised. "To which organizations?"

"Doesn't matter."

How am I supposed to figure out what makes him tick if he blows off every question I ask? "Humor me."

He leans forward, and finally I seem to have captured his attention. "The two main ones are Albright Literacy Foundation and King's Sports Grants."

Interesting choices. Not the cookie cutter variety. Also, literacy? This guy? I don't see it. King's Sports Grants makes more sense. They give scholarships to kids from low socioeconomic backgrounds to give them a chance to train with the best.

"Do you mentor any kids in the program?"

"Nah." He holds his hands up, palms facing me. "I'm strictly a hands-off guy."

Of course he is. My upper lip curls. I shouldn't have expected anything different. Still, he must have some redeeming qualities. Everyone does. "Do you volunteer your time anywhere?"

"No."

"Have any pets?"

"Nope."

Snapping the notebook shut, I slam it on the table. "Mr. Rawlins, I can't help you if you won't let me."

"Call me Jase."

"No, thank you." That suggests a level of familiarity I'm not comfortable with.

He scans me, and I feel every hair that isn't in place but resist the urge to smooth them down. "Do you volunteer, Lena?"

I shift in the chair, uncomfortable with the way he's looking at me. "This isn't about me."

"There." He sits back, smiling smugly. "See? You hate being interrogated too. It's an invasion of privacy."

"It's my job." And he's clearly not going to make it any easier. Time to try another tactic. "Do you mind if I shadow you for the rest of the day?"

Chapter 6

Scene 6

J ase

"Shadow me?" I ask in disbelief. "As in, follow me around? Go everywhere I go?"

Lena nods, tilting her head, a cascade of dark red hair spilling over her shoulders. It's beautiful, like liquid magma. I want to glide my fingers through the silky length, wrap it around my hands and pull it so her throat is bared to me. I admit to being fascinated by necks. They're the human body's most vulnerable point, with the jugular vein running just beneath the surface of the skin. Touching someone's neck is powerful. It can bring pain, or pleasure. I should know. After all, I'm famous for choking people into submission. But when women are in my bed, pain is the last thing they experience.

"That's the general idea, yeah," she says, unaware of the dirty thoughts swirling through my mind. "If you won't talk to me, it's the best way for me to get a feel for who you are."

I snort. "What do you care who I am?"

"I care because I'm paid to."

Ouch. Kitten has claws.

I can't see how her shadowing me is going to help, and having her nearby will distract me from training, but I consider the idea anyway. She probably thinks I live it up, snort coke out of groupies' navels and have orgies in my backyard. If she sees how boring I am, perhaps she'll leave me alone and do whatever it is she needs to tick off her bullshit boxes.

Really, there isn't much to know about me. I train, eat, sleep, and hang with my brothers. When I need to let loose, I call one of my casual hook-ups for a quick fuck. The girls I spend time with know the drill. Fighting comes first. We can be friends, but we're not ever going to be more. That suits them nicely, too. Who'd want to be the girlfriend of a professional MMA fighter? We're never around, have no time for anyone, and women throw themselves at us whenever we go out in public.

"Fine," I agree, and her brows hike up. "You can follow me back to the gym." As soon as she gets a load of the grungy, über-masculine place where I train, she'll want out. And if she doesn't, at least she'll provide some entertainment for the guys.

She stands. "Thanks."

I stand too, and the top of her head only reaches my chin. "You won't be thanking me soon. You're gonna be bored out of your mind."

For the first time today, she gives me a genuine smile. "Don't talk like you know me, fighter boy. I might surprise you."

"I hope you do." But I doubt it. "I'm parked out front. Is your ride nearby?"

She shakes her head. "I shouldn't be surprised you managed to get a prime park. Someone probably cleared it especially for you. Perks of the job, huh?"

Palms on the table, I lean forward. "I'm just that scary. All it takes is one look and everyone gets out of my way."

Her lips twitch. If I didn't know better, I'd think I amused her.

"I'm in a building nearby," she says. "I'll meet you there."

"You have the address?"

"Google. Duh."

Here I was thinking she'd looked me up. As if. She can't make her disdain any clearer. I gesture for her to precede me into the hall, then glance at her ass as she walks two steps ahead of me. It's heart-shaped and perky. Exactly the kind of ass I like. If only it didn't come attached to such a smart-mouthed package.

* * *

The parking lot at the gym is nearly empty this time of day, and though I hear music and thuds inside, no one else is around out here. Nick has left, having better things to do than babysit me, and I lean on the hood of my Camaro, ankles crossed, arms folded over my chest to combat the chill in the air.

Finally, a tiny electric Nissan pulls onto the asphalt and crawls to a halt beside me. Pushing off from the Camaro, I pace a circle around the Nissan while Lena messes with something in the glove compartment. Her car is shiny, as if it's just been washed, and it's well-kept. A sticker on the front windshield shows it was serviced this month, and when I peer through the window, the interior is immaculate too.

Is this girl human? My Camaro smells like used gym gear and has protein bar wrappers stuffed under the seats. That's how it should be. Lena's Nissan has no personality.

"Took you long enough," I say when she thrusts the door open and slides out, her heeled shoes clacking on the asphalt.

She swings a bag over her shoulder, nearly taking me out, and starts toward the gym entrance. "Not everyone gets special treatment. It took me fifteen minutes to get to my car."

"Hold up." I jog to catch her—she moves surprisingly fast in those shoes. When I touch her arm, she flinches and I drop my hand instantly. What's with that? I didn't take her for the jumpy type. Sassy and feisty, yes. Nervy, no. "Before you go in, we need to lay some ground rules."

She cocks her head and tries to smirk, but I can tell my touch has shaken her. "Go ahead. Lay down the law."

She's fishing for a reaction and I want to bite, but I resist. The less she gets from me, the sooner she'll be gone. Besides, I'm intrigued by her strange reaction. "Don't ask any questions. Don't distract the other guys. Their training time is precious. Keep off the mats, I don't want you getting hurt."

"So I should sit in the corner and not talk to anyone?" She wishes she could hit me. I can read the blood lust in her eyes and pray none of my brothers see fit to hand her a pair of gloves.

"Now you're getting it."

"I'll do my best not to mess up your training." She speaks through gritted teeth. "But I reserve the right to talk to people before they begin and after they're done."

"Fair." Probably as much as I can ask for. "Just so you know, it's nothing fancy."

"Jase." She meets my eyes. Holds the contact. Her earlier hesitation is gone. "I have been in a martial arts gym before. This isn't new to me."

"Oh, right. Go on, then."

When we enter, our eyes take a moment to adjust because the gym only has a few windows, located high enough on the walls that no one can break in. At least, not without some serious forethought. With the exception of a strip of concrete immediately inside the door, the entire floor is covered by alternating gray and black mats nearly an inch thick. At the far end is the octagon we practice in, and heavy black bags line the wall opposite the entry—some reaching the ground, some only for boxing, and a couple of speed bags for stamina and endurance.

I breathe in the scent of leather, liniment and sweat. It's so familiar to me. So welcoming. This place is home. Much more so than the fancy house I sleep in every night.

How does my favorite place look through Lena's eyes? Does she understand the pain and hard work that happens here? Does she appreciate the motivational quotes and words of wisdom scrawled on the walls by the fighters who train here, and the ones who came before us?

"All of these places smell the same," she remarks, dropping her bag and bending to remove those sexy shoes.

I kick off my sneakers and pad onto the mats. "Been in a few, have you?" I struggle to picture it.

"Enough."

It's a non-answer. I don't like that, but given how forthcoming I've been, I can't blame her. "Sit on one of those chairs over there." I wave my hand at them. "Hope you brought something to do."

"I'll keep myself occupied."

Grabbing my wraps from where they're airing out, I watch my brothers Gabe Mendoza and Devon Green sparring in the octagon as Seth stands below and shouts instructions. As usual, Devon is going a million miles an hour with a seemingly endless tank of gas, and Gabe is quietly countering and letting him wear himself out. A timer beeps and they slap each other on the back and leap out for a drink break.

I see the exact moment Devon looks up and spots Lena. A grin spreads over his face and he changes direction, his water bottle forgotten. He slings a towel around his neck, wipes the sweat off his face, then heads right for us.

"Hey, Jase," he calls. "Who's your friend?"

"I'm Lena," she says, before I have a chance to tell him to butt out. "Jase's new public relations rep."

Devon gives me a shit-eating grin. "Oh, really?" He offers her a hand. "I'm—"

"Devon Green," she interrupts, shaking his hand but looking unimpressed.

"Are you an MMA fan?" he asks, not deterred by the arctic chill she's sending his way.

"No."

"Then how—?"

"It's my job to know who's who in sports, Mr. Green."

Devon hoots with laughter. "Mr. Green!" He looks like she's made his day. "Can you believe that? I've never been called mister in my life." He yells to Gabe, "Get over here, asshole. Meet Jase's new PR woman." He turns his most charming smile on her, all flashing white teeth against mahogany skin. "Are you here to watch?"

She shifts in a way that makes me think she's uncomfortable and glances over his shoulder at Gabe, who's approaching with his usual expression. That is to say, stoic and difficult to read. "Yeah, that's the plan. I didn't mean to interrupt your session."

"Don't worry," I tell her, wrapping my hands with deft movements. "This isn't on you, it's on these nosy fuckers."

"Hey," Gabe grunts, watching her with those weirdly intense eyes of his. He's the brother of my soul, but if I didn't love the guy so much, he'd come across as a bit of a creeper. "You're the one who's going to fix this thing with Erin?"

Lena lifts her chin. "I'm going to try."

"Good." Gabe sticks his fist out and—to my complete astonishment—she bumps it. "That's all we can ask for. You need anything, sing out, okay? Dev and I will help in any way we can."

She shoots me a hard-edged look, as if to say, 'Hey, they're willing to help.' Of course they don't mind talking to her. It's not their livelihoods and years of work at risk. "Thanks, Gabriel."

Gabe cringes, his shoulders coming up to his ears. "Just Gabe, please. Gabriel was an angel. You won't find any of them around here."

"Noted."

"You want to join in?" This brilliant question comes from Devon. He's always the first to make nice with a pretty girl. Gabe is too focused to flirt, and me... well, frankly, I don't bother. It's usually unnecessary.

She scoffs and glances down at herself, drawing all of our attention to her tight skirt. "Do I look like I'm dressed to grapple?"

Devon's mouth hitches higher on one side. "You look just fine, Lena, but point taken. Don't rush off, we'll talk to you after."

She nods and sits in one of the chairs, primly crossing her legs and balancing a notepad on her knee.

"She is hot," Devon murmurs when we're halfway across the mats. "But you lucked out, bro, she doesn't like you. What'd you do?"

"Hit a girl," I mutter. "Supposedly."

"Ah, right."

"Yeah, she thinks I'm guilty."

Devon thumps my shoulder. The punch is solid, but I'm used to it and it barely rocks me. "Guess it's up to me and Gabe to scrap over her then."

"Go for your life." I don't think Lena is looking for a fighter boyfriend, and even if she is, the thought of Gabe fighting over a girl is laughable. His temper is so level, it's a miracle he can muster enough aggression to take his opponents down in the ring. Probably the only thing that would set him off is if someone messed with his best friend, Sydney.

Gabe ignores our exchange, hauling himself into the octagon. "It's king of the ring."

Seth, who's been pounding a bag, comes over, chest heaving. Our coach is a big dude, and like Gabe, he's not much for small talk. "Each time someone taps out, they swap with the third person. Jase, I want you shadowboxing in the corner until you're warm."

"Got it." I get out of the others' way and start skipping on the spot, flexing my calves, getting my blood flowing. Once the muscles are starting to burn, I raise my fists and throw a jab-cross at an invisible opponent, pivoting out of the way as I imagine them returning the blows. I stay light on my feet. Uppercut, hook, move.

And then I'm in the zone.

Chapter 7

Scene 7

L ena

The three guys have been sparring for ten minutes before their coach, a man in his late thirties or early forties and built like a freight train, sidles over and drops into the seat beside me. He watches them for a while, neither of us speaking. I sense he wants to talk, but this isn't the kind of man you can hurry into anything, so I wait patiently, my eyes on "Dangerous" Devon Green and Jase as they circle each other. Lightning fast, Devon's foot flies out and knocks Jase's legs out from under him. He crashes to the ground, then rolls back to his knees, and is up again like it never happened.

"Fast recovery," I remark. "That was a tidy sweep."

The coach turns and I can feel him appraising me, but I don't look around. "You know kickboxing?" he asks.

Finally, I give him my attention. His face looks like it's seen a few knocks, but he's a good-looking guy if you like the commanding military type. His reddish hair is shorn short, his eyes a bluish green, and his jaw is square and strong. "Only the basics."

"Never been in a ring yourself?"

The idea is so ludicrous, I laugh. "No, and I have no intention of changing that."

"But you'll happily date fighters?" His voice drips with disdain.

My jaw drops. So much for waiting for him to open up. It seems he's here to question me. "Excuse me?"

He doesn't look away, his eyes boring into mine. "I've seen you with Karson Hayes. Is he your boyfriend? Did he send you here to do recon?"

I'm so stunned, I sputter, at a loss for words. After a few seconds, I get a hold of myself. "I'm here because Jase hired me." Even if he hadn't been enthusiastic about it. "I used to date Karson, but we broke up." A shiver passes over me, despite the warmth of the gym. "It wasn't pretty."

"Ah." There's a wealth of understanding in that one word. "Don't judge us all harshly because of Hayes. A few bad seeds don't make all MMA fighters bad. Jase is a good guy."

Is he reading my mind? How can he possibly know that my past with Karson would prejudice me against Jase? But despite his insight, I'm not sure I believe him. So I settle for making a noncommittal sound and refocusing on the octagon.

"What's your name?" His voice is soft in my ear, like he knows he's hit a sore spot.

"Lena." At the opposite end of the gym, Jase tags Devon on the chin and ducks a retaliatory strike. "And yours?"

"Seth."

"Is this your gym?"

"Yeah." He spreads his legs wider and rests his forearms on them. The position brings him closer to my height. "Do me a favor, Lena. Bear with Jase. He may come off as all ego and hot air, but he's a decent person and he didn't do what Erin says he did."

Relief filters through me, intense and baffling. I shouldn't care one way or the other if he's guilty. He's a job, that's all. But Seth is the first person to outright proclaim his innocence, and for some reason, I'm glad that someone has. He's certainly not doing it himself.

Frustration chases on the heels of my relief. "Maybe he should come out and say that, then."

Seth shrugs. "He's not the type. He'd rather just get on with business and wait for people to stop talking."

The men in the ring swap around, Devon subbing out and Gabe subbing in. Jase goes for Gabe's legs, thudding his shin into the other guy's thigh. Gabe responds with a straight punch, and then pulls him in to grapple. It's easy to see how Gabe got his nickname, The Mind-Reader. He seems to anticipate each move Jase makes and responds fluidly, without hesitation. Over Gabe's shoulder, my gaze locks with Jase's. His eyes are hot and furious. I hear my own intake of breath, and feel Seth staring at me, but my attention is on Jase's stunning gray eyes.

Until it's not.

His ass hits the floor. Gabe sweeps his feet out from under him while he's distracted. Devon whoops from the sideline as Jase picks himself up, red in the face, and sneaks a look over at me. His expression is so mortified, I can't help but laugh.

Devon cackles louder. "You hear that, brother? You took a beating because of her, and she's laughing. That's cold, man."

I cover my mouth to hide my smile, but it's too late. The mortification fades from his face, though the flush lingers, and slowly, he sends me a crooked, sexy-as-hell grin.

Chapter 8

Scene 8

Jase

After the tripping incident, I manage not to embarrass myself in front of Lena again. The guys have seen me hit the mat more times than I can count, but when a gorgeous girl is watching, it's different. Maybe it's stupid, but I want to impress her.

When we finish, I grab a kettlebell and start a set of reps. Swings, squats, overhead raises, repeat. And repeat again. For fighting, it's important to strengthen my body using functional movements. Back when I first started, I spent hours benching and deadlifting as much as I could without killing myself, and all I ended up with was shitty cardio and a bulky body that seized up midway through sparring.

Yeah, maybe I'd looked like a gladiator, but it hadn't been worth it. I'm older now, and my ability to win ranks higher in my priorities than how shredded I look on weigh-in day. I'm into my third set of reps when Lena leaves her seat in the corner and pads across the mats toward me. Her feet are bare, and they're as white as the rest of her, with delicate toes and manicured nails. Why the hell am I noticing her feet?

"Can we talk more?" she asks, kneeling beside me so she can rest her notepad on her thigh. Having her on her knees is not helping my concentration.

I grunt. "I'm kinda busy." Training is the important thing now. Beating Karson is all that matters.

She taps her pen against the paper, impatient. "Come on, Jase. Seth told me you didn't assault Erin, but you have to give me something to work with or you're feeding yourself to the piranhas."

Of all days, Seth chooses this one to open his mouth? The fucker. Most days, trying to get anything out of him is like prying secrets from a CIA agent. "I need to train."

"I get that." She shifts onto her butt and tucks her legs to the side. "And I don't want to interfere, just give me something."

I finish a set of swings and move to squats again. Her eyes track my movements, and her pupils dilate when they reach my thighs and ass. Yeah, she's into me. Maybe she doesn't like it, but there's no denying the fact. I bet right now she's wondering how big my cock is, and whether it's proportionate to the rest of me. Good news, cutie pie: it is.

Not. Helping.

I need to think with my brain rather than my dick. And my brain knows that whatever motherhood-and-apple-pie story Seth sold her about me, she doesn't completely believe it. It will take more than sentimental words from a semi-retired fighter with the charm of a mountain lion to convince her of my innocence.

"Why should I tell you anything?" I demand, feeling sweat trickle down the back of my neck and soak into my top. The whole damn thing is drenched. Typical for me, but I'm beyond grateful I'm not one of those guys who stink when they sweat. I don't think I could handle her turning her perfect little nose up. "You've already made up your mind about me."

She sighs, and one of her hands goes to the edge of her skirt, toying with the hem. It's unconscious—she's not trying to tease me—but man, I want to peel it up and see what's beneath.

"My opinion doesn't matter."

"Yeah, actually, it does." Where did that confession come from? Her gaze snaps to mine, a gasp passing between her ruby red lips. Oh well, I'm the type to go big or go home. "It matters to me, Lena."

She holds my gaze for a long time, emotions warring in her eyes. I think I've gotten through to her, but then she shores up her defenses and says, "As if you care what I think. You're just messing with me."

Then she gets up and stalks off, her spine straight, shoulders stiff. Jeez, this girl really has issues, but for the first time, it occurs to me that maybe she's prickly for a reason. Maybe someone did a number on her. Someone like me. Perhaps that's why I rub her the wrong way. The thought makes me feel like a bastard for being hard on her.

"Bro," Devon calls as she slips on her shoes and makes for the door. "You gonna go after her, or what?"

I probably should. I lower the kettlebell to the mat and follow her out the exit, catching her just outside. "Hey, wait up."

She doesn't stop, although her step falters. I don't want to grab her and cause a scene—or give her a reason to join Erin in condemning me in the court of public opinion—so I jog around and block her path.

"Stop," I puff, holding up a hand. "I'm not trying to mess with you."

She quirks her brow in an 'are you for real' expression.

"Seriously. I just..." I sigh. "I get the feeling you don't like me, and it pisses me off because you don't even know me." She starts to interrupt, but I gesture for her to hold off. "I'm not finished yet. I don't want you to think I'm making excuses for myself, but my upcoming fight is a really big deal. I've been working toward it for years, and I need to keep my head in the game. If I let Erin mind-fuck me, then I'm a goner, and that's what she wants. She wants me to suffer because she tried to get me back and I turned her down. That's all this is. Revenge. I can't let her get to me. She won't press charges, she just wants to make me squirm."

Lena backs up a step, increasing the distance between us, but her eyes have softened and I think perhaps I see a glimmer of something other than dislike. "Jase."

I shiver. Fuck, I love my name in her mouth. I want to hear it when I'm driving into her. Unfortunately, that's unlikely to happen, and please God don't let her look down.

"You're right, I don't know you, or Erin, but even if you're being honest, I think you're underestimating the problem. Have you ever heard that saying about a woman scorned?"

I shake my head. "Doesn't count. There was never anything serious between us."

"Maybe Erin sees it differently."

That makes me pause and think. I picked Erin up at one of Devon's fights and knew from the outset that she wasn't interested in my heart or personality. Despite that, it was possible I'd read her intentions wrong and she'd wanted more than a casual fling—not because of any deep feelings but because of my money and pseudo-celebrity status. Some women like being able to lay claim to the biggest, baddest fighter available. Perhaps she wanted to be the one standing by my side, basking in the glory when I kick Karson's ass and win the championship belt.

I shrug. "It's possible."

She smiles, and it hits me like a liver punch. She's so damn radiant when she smiles, like the sun's shining out of her face. "I'm glad you're open to the idea."

"I'm not a total fuckwit."

"Never said you were."

She thought it though; she's crap at hiding her emotions. Slowly, so as not to scare her off, I take her by the shoulders and step closer, gazing into her eyes. Flecks of gold sparkle in their depths, and one day I plan to count them and figure out if they change depending on her mood. But not now.

"I meant what I said in there, Lena. For some godforsaken reason, your opinion matters to me. Do you believe I hit her?"

She sucks her lower lip into her mouth and glances down. "What I believe is irrelevant."

Bitter disappointment settles over me and I lether go, resisting the urge to kick the ground. I can't risk injuring my foot ata time like this. "Fine, then. Go."

Chapter 9

Scene 9

J ase

After jumping rope for an hour and doing so many burpees, I can't do another without face planting, I stand beneath the scorching shower in the gym's toilet block and wash a day's worth of sweat down the drain. My muscles tremble, and I rub the meaty parts of them, working out the lactic acid. Once I've soaped and rinsed off, I towel dry and spread liniment over my legs, arms, and shoulders. Smelling like menthol and aftershave—my usual scents, along with sweat and leather—I return to the gym and clap each of my brothers on the back, then collect my carbohydrate-enriched protein shake from the fridge and head to my car.

During the drive to the salon where Erin works, I drink the protein shake. I haven't told the others where I'm going because I don't need a lecture, or anyone standing in my way. Erin and I are overdue for a heart to heart. Parking a few blocks from the salon, I pull my hood up and speed walk the rest of the distance. I'm on a mission, and if anyone delays me, I might not arrive in time to catch Erin. She's not the type to work overtime.

As I walk, I wonder where "home" is for her these days. As far as I can tell, she only ever lives by herself for as long as it takes to find a new man who has a little fame and plenty of money. The name of the salon is written in pink script on the glass door, and pushing it open to enter feels plain wrong. The sign may as well read: girl zone, keep out.

I throw my hood back, then stuff my hands into my pockets. "I'm here to see Erin."

After eye-fucking me so thoroughly I need another shower, the receptionist calls out, "Erin, babe, there's someone here for you."

Erin turns from where she's trimming an elderly woman's hair and goes as white as her bleached blonde locks, fumbling with the scissors, which clatter to the floor—thankfully without removing any of her client's scalp.

"J-Jase," she stammers.

The receptionist's lust morphs to disdain. "This is the guy who gave you that black eye?"

I can't help but notice that the black eye is visible even across the room. Erin is more than capable of concealing it if she wants to, but she's enjoying the attention.

"Erin." I jerk my head toward the door. "Can I talk to you outside?"

Erin exchanges looks with several other women. One of them, who is painting a teenage girl's nails, advises her not to go with me. Frustration roars through me, but I tamp it down. Letting my temper get the better of me has never done any good when it comes to her. For someone who enjoys poking at people's vulnerable places, she doesn't like it when they poke back. Her mouth firms and she thrusts her chest out like she's about to enter a gladiatorial arena. I roll my eyes. How did I ever get past her attitude for long enough to find her attractive?

"Two minutes," she says, then reassures her colleagues with a quiet, "We'll be fine, girls. We'll stand in the window so you can see if I need help."

My jaw cranks impossibly tighter. She's making me out to be a monster, when all I'm guilty of is not being enough of a sucker to take her back. She sets aside her tools and brushes hair from the front of her pink blouse in an action intended to draw my gaze to her tits, which are exposed by a plunging V-neck.

The bruise around her eye is turning yellow-brown, and if anyone really thought about it, they'd see it's older than she claims, but no one is inclined to question her story. I wait for her to exit before following. I'm not stupid enough to leave first and let her lock me out. She leads me outside and when she turns to face me, her fearful expression has changed into smug self-assurance. She honestly believes this is going to play out how she wants. That I'll abide by her terms. She doesn't know me as well as she thinks she does.

She speaks first. "Hey, baby. You had time to think about my offer?"

I cross my arms. "My answer's the same as last time you asked. When are you going to quit this pathetic grab for the spotlight?"

"Pathetic," she spits, brown eyes blazing. "That's what everyone will think of you when I'm done." She sneers, and unlike with Lena, there's nothing sexy about it. "Whether or not you win the championship, you'll just be the chump who hits his girlfriends." Her lips curl up. "Even better, I could stop your championship fight. You can't compete from prison, Jase."

"I'm not giving in to you," I tell her. "I'm not taking you back, or giving you money just because you're blackmailing me." I've worked too damned hard to let a bitchy ex ruin my career. I've come a long way from the shitty neighborhood where I grew up, and I won't let a woman with an addiction to headlines get in the way. "Why don't you move on to the next guy? Surely there are heaps of other stupid fuckers out there who'll give you what you want."

Erin's hands drop from her hips and she crumbles in on herself. At first I think I've gotten through to her, but then I spot the guy across the road with a camera. She's playing the victim for a photographer. Fuck, just what I don't need.

"Know what, baby?" she asks, staring at the ground as though she's terrified of me, though her tone gives her away. She's loving this. Every fucking second of it. "I've had reporters calling me all day." Her eyes flick up and catch mine. "Even some from E News. Maybe I'll return their call. I've always wanted to be on TV."

"You do that, and you're never getting anything from me."

She flinches, like I've yelled at her. She's a piece of work, but she's a first rate actress. "Jase," she says softly, "I have nothing to lose."

She's got me, and she knows it. She has plenty to gain and I have everything to lose. Swearing, I turn and thump my fist into the wall. A light flashes.

Erin leaps away from me, wrapping her arms around herself. "You'll change your mind." She scuttles off, giving a damned good impression of a wounded puppy, and my heart sinks to the soles of my shoes. I played right into her plan, and I have a feeling I'll be facing the consequences tomorrow.

Hunching my shoulders, I pull the hood over my head and hurry away.

Chapter 10

Scene 10

Lena

Despite my best efforts to persuade Adrian to hand Jase Rawlins to another member of the team—because we clearly aren't a good fit for each other—Tuesday morning rolls around and I'm stuck with him. I'm on my second coffee of the day, a hazelnut mocha whip, when Breanna, my favorite person in the building, marches into my office and drops a tabloid on my desk.

I greet her with a smile. "Hey, Bree."

At a smidge over five feet, with flawless brown skin and more curves than an hourglass, Breanna is basically my opposite, except when it comes to levels of sass. In that, we're equal.

"You see the news, Lee?" she asks, wasting no time with pleasantries. Smoothing out the magazine, she points to the headline. "Your latest pet project won a front page spot. I hope you have an appetite for damage control because that's all that's on the menu today."

I lean over to get a better look at the headline, which reads, "Scared into silence? Jase 'The Wrangler' Rawlins stalks battered ex-girlfriend outside her workplace".

Oh. Fuck. No.

That idiot. That monumental, moronic, miniature-brained man. Champion fighter or not, I could kill him with my bare hands.

"Tell me he didn't," I say, going straight to the damning photograph of Jase towering aggressively over the petite blonde I know to be Erin Daley. The date in the corner shows it was taken yesterday. Shit. I scramble to order my thoughts. Breanna is right; this will take an act of God to counter, and I don't have a direct line to the man upstairs.

"That's one of three mags I've seen today with different takes on the same theme," Breanna tells me, sliding into the chair opposite and giving me time to read. It seems Jase took it upon himself to pay a visit to Erin at her work yesterday after I returned to the office. The article says he was overheard speaking to her with a raised voice and threatening her if she didn't keep silent.

I finish reading, flip it shut, close my eyes, and groan. "This is bad."

"Worse than any frat boy crap your usual clients pull," Breanna agrees. "What are you going to do?"

Straightening, I tug a hand through my hair, grateful I decided to wear it loose. "I don't know. Give me ten minutes, I need to think on it."

She eyes me dubiously. "Don't take too long. You need to start putting out those fires."

"I know." I've been trying to put out fires ever since Jase Rawlins sauntered into my life, and it seems like I'm only adding fuel to the flames. Was it my conversation with him that prompted him to confront his ex? God, I hope not. "On second thought, sitting around here isn't going to fix anything." Standing, I shove my chair back and grab my purse. "I'm going to track him down and demand to know what the hell he was thinking."

"Atta girl." She slaps my butt as I pass her on the way out. "You tell that big alpha fighter how it is, Lee."

"Oh, I plan to."

Jase Rawlins doesn't know what's about to hit him. Fuming, I make my way through the office and give the stink-eye to the cute security guard when he tries to flirt with me, then stomp all the way to my car. It's a good thing I've been wearing heels since the same age I developed boobs, otherwise I'd have broken an ankle by now. The drive to Crown MMA Gym only worsens my mood because I hit traffic the moment I leave the parking building and it doesn't let up the whole way, giving me plenty of time to stew.

Pausing, I reapply my lipstick and smooth my hair, which, thanks to my nervous habit of messing with it, is no longer sleek and professional. Satisfied I don't look as frazzled as I feel, I snatch the magazine from the passenger seat and stalk across the asphalt. Someone whistles, and I snap around, my gaze landing on a guy who's leaning out of a car window. I flip him the bird.

"Aw, don't be like that," he calls, but I step inside and slam the door.

A dozen men swivel to face me, possibly curious who has the audacity to interrupt their workout. Most of them resume training a few seconds later, but Jase's eyes widen and he falls back a step. Gabe is holding pads for him, and he gives me a slight nod. I start forward, only remembering to remove my shoes at the last moment. When I try to tug them off, the buckle-up pumps don't cooperate, and I have to sit, my skirt riding up my thighs. Both Jase and Gabe watch the show without offering to help. Jackasses. Finally free of the shoes, and unfortunately several inches shorter, I cross to them and slam the magazine against Jase's chest.

"Want to tell me what the hell you werethinking?"

Chapter 11

Scene 11

J ase

All the frustration I've worked off over the past two hours comes flooding back at the sight of Lena—furious expression, sassy walk, and all. Her cheeks are flushed with anger and her eyes may as well be shooting laser beams straight at me. Her lips move, but I don't hear the words. My blood has redirected from my big head to my generously proportioned smaller one. Fuck, she's hot when she's mad.

She thumps me in the chest, and I scarcely notice. Her fists are tiny. She could probably punch me in the nose and not even crack the bone. Her eyes narrow, and she gets up in my face—a hard ask when she's several inches shorter than me.

"Do you think this is funny?" she asks, jabbing me in the chest with her free hand. I glance down and see she's holding a magazine. With a sinking sensation, I take it from her and hold it up so I can see the cover. It's a photograph from yesterday, of me standing over Erin like a brute. The headline screams at me, and I show Gabe, then shove the magazine into Lena's hands, sick to my stomach. I won't read it.

I already know it's full of vitriolic bullshit, and I don't even blame the reporter for spouting it. I handed the media a gold mine by going after Erin. I've made her the poster child for standing up in the face of domestic abuse, with me cast in the role of monster.

Jesus. Fuck.

Lena was right all along. This is serious.

"There are others," she says, in case I'm holding out any hope that the story has been picked up by a lone tabloid. Closing my eyes, I mutter a stream of curses, growing more creative with each one.

"Hey, brother." Gabe claps me on the shoulder, which nearly knocks me over since his forearms are covered by heavy kick pads. "You can get past this." He turns to Lena. "You can fix this, right? That's what he hired you for?"

Lena releases a long, slow breath. I can sense her hesitation, and it fuels a desperation deep within me. I worked fucking hard to get to where I am. It's not possible that a selfish girl with a taste for the spotlight could take it away so easily, is it?

"Please." I grab her free hand between both of mine even though she has a perfect manicure and my gloves are soaked with sweat and completely disgusting. "You've gotta try."

She stares at me, some of her hostility fading, and nibbles on her lower lip. Finally, an excruciatingly long moment later, she says, "You just made my job so much more difficult. I hope you understand that."

"I do."

"Trust me, Lena," Gabe adds. "He may come across as a douche, but he's not a stupid one. He knows he fucked up." He shucks his pads and stands shoulder to shoulder with me, the both of us facing her down. This doesn't seem to intimidate her as it might others. It fires her up. She flicks her sexy red hair over her shoulder and gives us a single, firm nod.

"Well, okay then. Glad we know where we stand." There's a brief moment when I think she's going to move on without rubbing salt in the wound. Then the moment passes. "For the record, I've met mushrooms with more forethought than you."

Should have known she wouldn't let me off so easily. I suppose if she wants to compare me to fungi, at least it's a tasty one.

"If we're going to do this, you need to be a whole lot more open with me. I want no-holds-barred access to your life, Jase. I ask a question, you answer it immediately and truthfully. I make a suggestion, you do everything within your power to make it happen. If you want to climb out of this hole you've dug, I need your complete and total commitment. Think you can manage that, fighter boy?"

"That's fighter man to you." I can't resist needling her, and her face screws up the way I knew it would. "But yeah, I'll do what you say and I'll accept any help I can get."

"Good." Her lips purse, and she seems to have run out of steam. I can see her mentally switching from bulldozer mode to thinking mode, calculating our next steps, figuring out how to get ahead of this, and for the first time, I feel like maybe she's on my side. Maybe she's actually invested in me.

The next question out of her mouth is one I don't see coming. "Is there any truth to Erin's story?"

"No," Gabe and I answer at the same time.

"Okay," she nods, accepting our reply at face value, and I can still see the information running through her mind and being processed. She has a shit poker face, but that's beside the point. This woman is actually listening to what I have to say and taking it on board. Is she for real?

Her belief in me—if that's what it is—feels good. Like, unreasonably good. I want to grab her around the waist and twirl her in the air, or take her face between my palms and kiss her irresistible ruby lips. When another ten seconds pass without her saying anything snarky, I'm halfway tempted to strip her clothes off and bang her on the floor, audience be damned.

Finally, she comes to a decision. "There are some things I need to take care of. I'll be in touch with you later."

Her hand is still in my grasp, and I squeeze it. "Thanks." My voice is raspy with emotion, and I cough to clear it. Goddamn it, I am not a pussy.

She studies me, and I'm not sure what she sees, but she seems to like it. "You're welcome, fighter man."

My lips quirk up. "You know what I think?"

She tugs her hand away and places it on her hip. "Do I want to know?"

Ah, there's my mouthy girl. "I think you like me." She starts to scowl, but I barrel on. "I think you care what happens to me."

"Do not," she says, a deep blush traveling down to the neckline of her shirt. With a complexion like that, I bet her entire body blushes, and I want to tear her blouse in half to find out. "I care about keeping my career on track."

"Uh-huh." I give her a cocky grin that I know will rile her more. "You tell yourself that, cutie pie."

She huffs. "You're insufferable." Then she whirls around and marches away, the curve of her butt bouncing with each step.

When she's gone, Gabe whistles under his breath. "Man, she's something."

I punch him in the gut, hard enough to sting but not hurt. "Eyes to yourself. She's not here for your viewing pleasure."

He guffaws. "That doesn't stop you."

"I don't need you pointing out my hypocrisy." I stretch my legs and shake them, refusing to analyze why the thought of anyone else checking Lena out makes me want to wrap my arm around the asshole's throat—friend or not. "Let's get back to training."

Chapter 12

Scene 12

Lena

I find Erin Daley at the salon where she works—incidentally, the same place Jase tracked her down to yesterday. After my conversation with him and Gabe, I'm fired up and determined to get to the bottom of this. I'm not certain I believe what he said about being entirely innocent, but I'll admit he was convincing, and I want to know, once and for all, what actually went down between him and his ex. I need to hear her side of the story and weigh it against his. Once I've deduced the truth—which I don't doubt I'll be able to do—I can decide on our next steps. Guilty or not, it's my job to help Jase, but I'll need to tread more carefully if I discover there's any truth to the accusations against him.

Entering through a glass door painted with pink script, I pause and look around. The salon is nice, probably out of my budget, with high ceilings and shiny surfaces for all the beautiful customers to admire themselves in. An array of expensive hair and skin products occupies the shelves beside the receptionist's desk, and I scan the labels, wishing I could afford to take a few bottles home with me.

"Can I help you?" the receptionist asks politely.

"I'm looking for Erin," I say, scanning the room, my gaze landing on Jase's ex as she paints dye onto a young woman's hair.

"Do you have an appointment?"

"No." I turn back to the receptionist. She's pretty, wearing a pale pink blouse, emblazoned with the logo of the salon. "I was hoping for a private moment with her. It'll only take a couple of minutes."

She lifts an appointment book onto the desk and runs a fingernail down the page. "Sorry, hon, she's booked full today."

Leaning closer, I drop my voice, hoping I sound like a gossipy airhead rather than the astute professional I generally prefer to be perceived as. "It's about her ex, the MMA fighter? I'm hoping to get a few words."

"Oh," she replies, a wealth of understanding in her tone. Even though I haven't technically lied, she's mistaken me for a reporter and I'm happy for her to continue under that impression. "In that case, if you wait for five minutes she'll be finished with her client and take a short break."

"That's perfect. I'm happy to wait." I smile like she's made my day. "Thank you for being so understanding."

"No problem. I'm just glad that asshole is paying for what he did." She props her elbow on the desk and rests her chin in it, her face only inches from mine. "Did you know he came here yesterday? I mean, the nerve." She tuts. "It's always the hot ones who turn out bad."

I laugh, and this time it isn't the slightest bit fake. "Trust me, I know." We exchange a conspiratorial look, one hard-done-by single woman to another. "I wish the looks made up for the personalities."

Although with Karson, it had been more than his personality that led me to end things so swiftly and decisively. The fucker had thought he could punch me and I'd stay with him. I was smart enough not to fight back at the time—the guy is a pro—but sometimes I regret that I didn't key his car or smash a window in his ridiculous mansion of a home.

"Hey, some are just boring," she says, drawing me out of my thoughts. "And a boring hot guy isn't so bad."

I nod in agreement, straighten and gesture to the sofa just inside the door. "I'll just wait over here."

"Go right ahead, hon."

Ten minutes pass before Erin joins me. I flip through one of the magazines on the coffee table and listen to the chatter in the salon. When she reaches me, I ask if there's somewhere private we can talk. She smiles, looking far more pleased with herself than I expect, and leads me out the back to a staff kitchenette.

The bright indoor lighting emphasizes the ugly mottled skin around her eye and the puffiness in one corner where it's swollen partially shut. It occurs to me that for a woman with a lot of makeup on—lipstick, brow pencil, eyeliner, mascara—she doesn't have any over the bruise. I wonder if that's because it hurts to apply makeup there, or whether she enjoys the attention it attracts. If Jase is to be believed, it's the latter, but my natural inclination is to assume the former. After all, I know better than anyone how much a man's fist can hurt.

"You wanted to talk to me about Jase?" she asks, and there's a glint in her eye I don't like. It's greedy. Excited. "Where are you from?"

"Actually," I say, "I work for Bolton & Symes Public Relations. My name is Lena. I've already heard Jase's side of the story, and I'd like to hear yours."

Her expression sours, her lips flattening and her eyes narrowing. "You work for Jase."

"No, I work for Mr. Bolton and Ms. Symes," I correct, sitting on a chair and indicating she should take the one beside me. "Why don't you tell me what went down, Erin?"

"I thought you were a reporter," she says, not moving. She doesn't want to join me, and it rubs me the wrong way that she was so willing to speak to a journalist but doesn't want anything to do with me. Perhaps she thinks I'm trying to sweep her problem under the carpet.

"I'm not. But I am someone who'd really like to hear what you have to say. Why don't you sit and start at the beginning?" I wave a hand at the seat. "I promise, I'm not here to harass you. Just to learn the truth."

Reluctantly, she sinks into it, giving me the side-eye as though I've tricked her, and crosses her legs, her miniskirt riding up.

"Jase hit me," she says with a shrug of one shoulder, studying the lining of the chair. "What else is there to say?"

I take my notebook and pen from my purse. "Was it just once, or was it a pattern?"

She shrugs again. "Just once." Looking up, she catches my eye. "It was terrifying."

I make a note of her answer. "Did he often lose his temper with you?"

"Oh yes, all the time." She's warming to the questions now, a smile flitting at the corner of her lips.

"And when he did, what would happen?"

"He'd yell, swear, sometimes throw things." She licks her lips like she has a particularly scandalous tidbit to share and leans toward me. "Once, he punched a hole in a wall."

I picture the massive, leanly muscled guy from the gym smashing a wall in a fit of rage and shiver. It's a frightening image. But it also doesn't gel with what I've seen of him. He's cocky and mouthy, but though he's certainly pouted plenty, he hasn't laid a finger on me in any way that's given me a legitimate reason for concern.

"That must have scared you," I say, to keep her talking.

Her eyes widen, then she winces, and I feel a pang of sympathy. "You have no idea."

I duck my head closer to hers, inviting her confidence. I get the impression she's a born storyteller, and loves having an audience. "Why did you stay with him?"

"Well... I..." She flounders, and I push away the urge to help her. I can't baby this woman if I want to get to the bottom of things. "I guess..." She gives an awkward laugh. "He's so fucking hot, you know? And he's not always a bad guy. Sometimes he was nice to me."

He's hot? That's her first response?

This is Vegas. There are thousands of hot guys out there if that's all that matters to her. Her answer doesn't ring true, and I want to poke it and see how she unravels.

"What happened the day he hit you?"

"We were dancing at a club. Flashlight—you might have heard of it." Her voice is strong and sure now; she's back on familiar ground. How many times has she told this exact same story? The words sound rehearsed, like they've been repeated over and over. I suppose she would have told whichever news outlet she originally spoke to, and probably her friends and colleagues, too. Still, something about her seems too... polished. If I didn't know better, I'd think she was bragging by name-dropping the hottest new club in town, which is next to impossible to get into.

"I've heard of it," I confirm.

Her face drops in disappointment, and I wonder if she was hoping I'd be more impressed by her glamorous lifestyle. "It's like, the place to be," she continues. "I was so freaking excited when he asked me to go with him. We had a few shots, and he went to the bathroom." At this point, it occurs to me that Jase told me he doesn't drink during fight camps, and I'm inclined to believe him. I wonder if it's a slip of the tongue, or if Erin just lied. I don't interrupt though, I want to see where she's going with this.

"I was dancing by myself and this other guy started hitting on me. I didn't lead him on," she says, tossing her perfect blonde hair in such a way that makes me think that's exactly what she did. "But when Jase got back, he went totally nuts. Like, more angry than I'd ever seen him before." Her lips twist in a smirk. "I guess he didn't like seeing someone else's hands on me. So he shoved the guy away, and it was such an alpha move"—at this point, she sighs dreamily—"so hot, and I just wanted to jump him, so we took a taxi home but he was in a crappy mood and when we were alone, he hit me and told me never to flirt with anyone else again. Then he got drunk, and he's a mean drunk, so I packed a bag and snuck out."

My brows shoot up. "You were living with him?"

This was a fact no one had mentioned.

"Ah, no." She colors, and drops her eyes. "I just left a few things there. Changes of clothes, you know."

"Stuff that you were worried enough about to go and collect when your boyfriend with an anger problem had just hit you?"

As someone who's been in that situation, I can attest that my personal belongings were the last thing on my mind. I just wanted to get somewhere safe and be held by someone who cared about me. I know that everyone reacts to situations differently, but this whole conversation seems off to me.

Erin is flustered now. The flush has spread over her entire face and her movements have become jerky. She shakes her head. "He was starting to calm down. I wasn't in any danger—"

"But you said he was a mean drunk," I point out.

Like someone slipping on a mask, Erin's expression changes. Her lips curl, her eyes become icy, and her hands still. The effect is like being doused with cold water. Forget innocent victim, the person in front of me is a straight-up mean girl.

"I don't know what you're insinuating, but I've had enough of this conversation. I'm going to tell anyone who'll listen what he did, and I'll probably have him arrested. Nothing you do or say will stop me." She stands, her back ramrod straight. "If Jase wants to talk to me, he can come here himself rather than sending his little messenger." Her sneer could have been taken directly from my high school nightmares. "I don't have to justify myself to you. You can see yourself to the door."

My temper flares and I get to my feet. "What's your play? You want him to come here so someone can take his picture and slam him all through the tabloids again? Because it won't work. I'm going to keep him far, far away from you." If it's the last goddamn thing I do.

She looks up at me because I'm taller than her, which is the only satisfactory thing about this situation. "As if you could."

"What's that supposed to mean?"

She steps closer, her hands on her hips, not the slightest bit intimidated by my height. "Jase is mine, bitch. You're just some girl on his payroll, so don't go thinking you actually mean anything to him. Desperation is not a pretty look on you."

All snappy comebacks desert me, and I gape at her. Is she for real?

"I don't want him," I tell her. "And even if I did, why the hell would you after what you've supposedly been through?"

She cocks her head. "I forgive him. That's what love is about."

"You forgive him, but you're planning to have him arrested?" This woman is deluded. Completely fucking nuts. And I'm beginning to think I got Jase all wrong. However it might appear, I'm not so sure Erin is the victim in this bizarre scenario.

"He needs a push." She bares her teeth. "Now get your skanky ginger ass out of my salon."

Chapter 13

Scene 13

J ase

I meet Lena for dinner at a salad bar. She's waiting at a table, sipping from a glass of water when I arrive. Her lips leave a scarlet ring on the rim of the glass and I can't help but think they'd leave a similar mark on my cock. She's in the same outfit she wore earlier, whereas I've showered and changed into jeans and a t-shirt—the type that's tight over my shoulders and abs. This isn't a date, but damned if it doesn't feel like one. I can't even remember the last time I sat down for a meal with a woman who wasn't dating one of my brothers. Well, except Sydney, Gabe's best friend, who's a hell of a girl and an honorary member of the team. We all know if any of us so much as looked at Sydney sideways, Gabe would rip our throats out.

Lena, on the other hand, I can look at as much as I please. And fuck yeah, I look. My eyes practically feast on her. She's crazy sexy, and it's been a couple of months since I was with a girl so I'm suffering the effects of the attraction because of my self-induced dry spell. I don't have many superstitions, but having a woman in my bed during a training camp is bad mojo, and that's a fact. Tried and tested.

"Stop eye-fucking me and sit down," she says, with no heat behind the words. "I'm starving. I want to eat."

Sliding into the chair opposite, I give her a slow, lazy grin. "I like a girl with an appetite."

She rolls her eyes. "Do you flirt every time you breathe?"

"Only with you, cutie pie." I don't need to check the menu because this place is one of my regulars. I eat free here three times a week, and in return I wear their logo and talk them up on social media. I gesture around the room. "What do you think? Surprised a meathead like me would choose a salad bar?"

"Not at all." She takes another drink, leaving more of her lipstick on the glass. "I know how well MMA fighters need to eat. My ex was one."

Huh. That takes the wind out of my sails. She looks at me like she expects me to ask about the ex, but frankly, I don't want to know. The thought of her being with another guy leaves a bad taste in my mouth.

"Speaking of exes." She sets the glass down and wipes her lipstick off with a napkin. "I talked to yours."

A lump forms in my throat, my mouth goes dry and I grab her glass and gulp the water, desperately wanting to know how her conversation with Erin went while also dreading the answer with every fiber of my being.

Her forehead furrows with annoyance, and her nose crinkles. "Get your own."

It feels strangely intimate sharing her drink. I have no regrets. "Yours tastes better. Is your lipstick flavored?"

She crosses her arms and glares at me. "It's cherry. Now can I have my water back?"

I shove it over to her, and under her careful watch, pour from the table pitcher into an empty glass. "You were saying?"

She huffs, and it's so cute I want to eat her up. God, I like it when she's flustered, and I like it even more when she gives me lip. Is anything about Lena not appealing?

"As I was saying, I had a chat with Erin." Her cheeks flame, and I wish I could see what's running through her mind. "She's a piece of work. What did you ever see in her?" I start to reply, but she holds a hand up. "Wait, I don't want to know. I can probably guess."

There's that snarkiness again. I wonder what she and Erin discussed. Did they talk about me? Whatever it is, it seems to have ruffled her feathers. I want to ask if she's jealous, because if she were anyone else, I'd think she resented Erin, one female to another, but I don't dare raise the question. At least, not yet.

"And?" I prompt.

"And," she continues dutifully, "I may have misjudged you. I'm sorry for that."

"You... what?" She's apologizing to me? "Is there a hidden camera somewhere? Are you punking me, Lena?"

She scowls. "No. I'm trying to behave like an adult. I seem to revert to teenage levels of maturity around you, but I want to do better. I made a mistake, and I'm not afraid to admit it. You're not the loser I thought you were."

Her admission is music to my ears. I wish I'd recorded it, to replay again and again. I never expected her to be so honest with me. If I'm being real, I thought she was too snooty for that, but perhaps she's not the only one of us guilty of misjudging the other.

"Thank you," I reply, letting her hear my sincerity. There's a time for being a dick and now isn't it. "That means more to me than you know."

"Yeah, well." She shrugs self-consciously. "No one is perfect."

Her lips press together, and fuck, I want to kiss them. The table is narrow, and if I lean across it, I could easily touch my mouth to hers. But if I did, it wouldn't be enough. I'd want to haul her onto my lap and grind myself into her ass. Would she ride me? Let her tongue tangle with mine and kiss me back with all that pent up fire inside her?

"Jase." Her voice is low and cautious. "Stop looking at me like you're hungry, and I'm dinner."

"I am hungry," I confess. "And not just for dinner. You look better than anything on the menu."

She wets her lips, and a breath escapes between them. Her eyes are dark, the blue just a pale ring around her enlarged pupils. Reaching over, I touch her hand, but she snatches it away. A shiver runs through her body, and I harden, imagining how hot it would feel to be inside her.

"You want me, too," I murmur, watching her try to pull herself together.

Her voice is raspy when she says, "We need to focus on work."

Sitting back, I let her change the topic, noticing she hasn't told me I'm wrong.

Chapter 14

Scene 14

L ena
I didn't realize it was possible to get so turned on just from hearing a growly alpha male make crude comments across the table in a salad bar. The fact there are people all around us—including children—barely registers. All I know is that he wants me, and I want him, and my single-minded vagina is throbbing between my thighs, begging for attention. Squeezing my legs together, I try to stop my thoughts from veering into the dangerous territory of wondering how Jase's stubble would feel against my skin.

Ugh, it must be morally wrong for me to be this horny in public. I'm already wet and ready for him, and all he's done is touch my hand. I'm not even sure I like the guy, even if he's not the violent asshole I initially believed.

"Lena?" His cocky grin widens, showing his teeth. He knows exactly what he's doing to me, the dick.

"Work," I say out loud. "Questions." Yes, that's it. "Will you answer more of my questions now?"

He sighs, and runs a hand over his damp hair. "There are things I'd rather do, but shoot."

Resorting to my notepad, I'm about to read the first item when a waitress comes to take our order. I choose a chicken salad tortilla, but Jase orders three separate meals without checking the menu.

"You come here often?" I ask when the waitress leaves.

"Yeah, they sponsor me, so I get free meals."

"Sweet deal."

He nods to my list. "What do you wanna know?"

A flock of pigeons take up residence in my belly. Now that I know Jase more, asking these questions feels personal. "You must earn a reasonable amount." I looked up his net worth earlier. Even if the estimate I found is a little off, it's impressive. "What do you do with your money?"

The question seems to bore him. He takes a drink from my glass again, even though his own is full. "I bought a house. I pay the bills and the mortgage. I see a physio and a massage therapist every week."

Nothing surprising there. "You mentioned yesterday that you contribute to charity."

"Yeah." He clams up. "Not much to say as far as that goes."

"Really?" I cock my head. "Are we back to one-word answers and evasion?"

He sighs, and rolls his neck from side to side. Finally, he speaks. "Most of my money goes to King's Sports Grants. I'm one of their major donors."

Because I'm a sadistic bitch who enjoys his discomfort, I ask, "Is there a particular reason for that?"

His neck cracks, and he rubs it, but his slate gray eyes catch on mine. There's something dark and unfathomable in their depths, and I can't look away. "If not for those grants, I'd probably be in jail by now."

Oh. This man gets more fascinating with every tidbit I tease out of him. "Why?"

He shrugs those massive shoulders, and glances behind me. A moment later, the waitress deposits a number of bowls in front of us. Each of Jase's meals is twice the size of mine, but I'm not surprised he can tuck away food like no one's business. He must burn through thousands of calories each day, and maintaining that muscle mass can't be easy. He grabs a fork and shovels lean beef and quinoa into his mouth while I wait patiently for him to answer.

"I grew up dirt poor," he mutters, looking like he'd rather be having any other conversation. He's much more confident when he's on the offensive, especially if that involves suggestive comments and glances hot enough to burn. "Went through the foster system. Never stayed anywhere long, but one of my foster fathers ran an MMA gym, and I picked it up easy. Got one of those grants so I could carry on after I moved. At my second fight, I met Seth, who runs Crown MMA. He was a big name at the time, and he took me under his wing. When I aged out of the system, I lived with him until I could afford my own place." He looks up and stares at me, as though daring me to look away. I don't. "There you have it. The sad story of Jase Rawlins."

"Not so sad," I say, taking a bite of chicken. "It's a rags to riches success story. America's favorite." When his eyes narrow, I add, "I'm sorry for how you grew up, though. That can't have been easy. For some reason, I pictured you as a spoiled rich kid."

This time, he laughs, and breaks away from our stare-down. "You probably saw me that way because it suited you."

I can't disagree, and for a while, we eat in companionable silence. When he finishes his beef salad, he takes a break before moving onto the next bowl.

"So what about you? What's your story, Lena?"

The way he says my name like a caress drives me crazy, and I resist the urge to shiver. "We're not talking about me."

He grins. "Maybe we should be. It's only fair that you spill all your secrets if you want to know mine."

I shake my head. "It's not an interesting story. The opposite of yours, actually. Grew up rich, refused to settle down with a nice boy like my parents wanted, paid my own way through college, and now I live in a tiny apartment I can hardly afford because I'm drowning in student debt."

"Huh." His brows draw together. This clearly isn't the story he expected, either. "But you look so"—he waves a hand at me—"put together."

A laugh-snort escapes me, and I bury my face in my hands. "Oh, my God." I can't believe I just made that sound in front of him. I might actually die of humiliation. "I only look put together." I keep my face in my hands. "It's my job to appear that way."

"So others trust you to make them look good, too?"

"Exactly."

"Lena." He touches my chin with a slight but firm pressure. "Look at me."

I raise my head and find him watching me intently, hunched forward so his gorgeous eyes aren't far from mine. "Yeah?"

"Your laugh is fucking cute."

I laugh-snort again—a nervous reaction—then groan. "It is not."

"Is too."

Straightening, I try to preserve what's left of my dignity. "We should stop arguing like kindergartners over something that doesn't matter."

His gaze pins me to the spot, and I'm unable to move. Hardly able to breathe. "I know you're not a kindergartner, Lena."

Why does he keep saying my name? Does he know how crazy it drives me?

Danger zone. Get back to business.

Shaking off the effect of his statement, I raise my glass, only remembering when it touches my lips and his pupils dilate that he's just been drinking from it himself. Forget danger zone, I'm heading into the territory of screwed beyond redemption.

"So..." I say slowly, gathering my wits from a puddle on the floor. "What else do you do with your spare time? Is there anything I need to worry about coming out of the woodwork?"

Jase draws back and continues eating his second salad. I'd think he was ignoring me, except his brow is furrowed in thought. "You shouldn't have anything to worry about." He polishes off the salad in a few massive mouthfuls and moves to the third, which looks like a mound of seasoned potatoes. "I used to be a party boy, can't deny that, but I didn't get to where I am by being that guy. I rarely drink anymore, don't do drugs, and don't fuck around indiscriminately. Haven't done that for a couple years."

My mind catches on that last part. "I thought all MMA fighters fucked around. Isn't that part of the code, or something? All those hot girls throwing themselves at you must be hard to resist."

His gaze flickers up and locks on mine as he chews. When he's finished, he swipes my water and drinks, his throat pulsing. "Didn't say I always resist, but I don't jump into bed with just anyone."

I have a feeling I won't like hearing what comes next, but I need to know anyway. "Elaborate."

"I have a few girls I hook up with when I'm not in fight camp." He shrugs. "They use me, I use them, and we all leave happy."

For some insane reason, the thought of these anonymous girls being with Jase makes me want to hunt them down and scratch their eyes out. He must read something in my expression because one side of his mouth hitches up.

"Pull your claws in, kitty. I don't have sex during fight camp, so I haven't been with anyone for a couple of months."

I gape. A couple of months? For a guy like him, that's an eternity. I expected him to have a different woman in his bed every weekend. Jesus, he must be wound tight. I bet all it would take is a few well-placed touches to make him desperate... and the thought of having this big man under my power is seductive as hell.

Not appropriate. He's a client, and a fighter. He's not for you. Keep your hands to yourself.

"Why?"

"Superstition. Most sportsmen have their share of idiosyncrasies. Surely you know that."

"Yeah, but the spoiled football players I usually deal with wouldn't go a week without a woman. If they could score two or three at once, they'd yell it from the rooftops."

"Football players." He pulls a face. "That's who you usually work with?"

"Football players, hockey players, and the odd basketball player." None of them remotely as unsettling as Jase.

He grins. "I bet they don't have a clue what to do with a girl like you."

I smile back. "They like to think they could try."

Jase reaches over and envelops my hand with his, his thumb drawing swirls on my palm. "If I had the chance, I'd know what to do with you."

I gulp. I don't doubt it for a moment, but I shouldn't encourage him, either. Even if he's a decent guy for the most part, he's still capable of violence, and what's more, the company has a policy against fraternizing with clients. Considering it's our job to protect their image, engaging in intimate activities with them is out of the question.

"So." My voice comes out as a squeak, and I cough to clear it. "What do you do when you're not training?"

Reading my cue to back off, he resumes eating. "I watch fight videos with my brothers for research, and coach the kids at my old community center."

"I didn't know you had brothers."

"Yeah, that's what I call the guys at the gym. They're the closest thing to a family I've ever had."

My heart melts a little at that. "Sweet."

"Sweet is the last thing I am, cutie pie."

Somehow, I think that's a lie. "You coach at a kids' program?"

"Yep." I've barely finished my meal while he's just demolished the potatoes. "I set it up at the community center in my old neighborhood. Just to give the kids an outlet for their anger, and someplace to go for a while where they don't have to worry about anything other than giving me their full attention, you know. There's no financial or racial divide in my group. It's a safe space for them."

Much as the idea of an MMA class being a "safe place" is bizarre, I can see it. I bet the kids adore him. And this is exactly the sort of thing I can use to dig him out from beneath the steaming heap of dung Erin piled on him.

"That sounds wonderful. They're lucky to have you." I can't believe how much I totally misjudged this guy. I suppose he was right, I wanted him to be a loser so I could write him off. "When's your next class? I'd like to come."

He scowls, forking the last piece of potato a little too violently. "I guess you want to take photos of me with the kids and get them to say how great I am, or some shit like that."

Gritting my teeth so I don't cuss him out for referring to my job as "some shit like that," I say, "Yes, that's about the sum of it. So, when is it happening?"

"Tomorrow. Five-thirty. At the Alderton Community Center." He shoves away his final plate. "But I don't want you exploiting those kids. They're vulnerable, and they come to the center for an escape."

I hold up my hands. "I won't exploit them. Promise. You can okay anything I write ahead of time, and you have veto rights."

His shoulders heave as he exhales. "Okay, then. Sounds like we'll be seeing each other again tomorrow."

My stomach fills with butterflies at the prospect, and I try to ignore them. The waitress returns with our bill and hands it to Jase. I grab my purse, but he signs something and sends her away.

"What was that about?" I ask.

"Taking care of dinner," he says. "You're my plus one, so you're covered under my sponsorship."

Nuh-uh. I wave my purse at him. "You're my client, not my date. I pay my own way."

"Not today, cutie pie."

"But—"

He stands, and the squeal of chair legs on the floor cuts me off. "Just give me this, Lena. You can pay next time."

"There's not going to be a next time," I mutter, hoping to God his paying for my dinner doesn't have anything to do with my confession about being broke. I'm no one's charity project.

"You tell yourself that." His hand lands in the small of my back as he guides me outside. "Where are you parked?"

I gesture up the street. "Over that way."

"I'll walk you."

"Not necessary."

He grabs me by the shoulders and spins me to face him. My brain ceases to function. I can't process even the most basic thought with his hands on me like that.

"Babe, when a man wants to see you safely to your car, you let him. Unless he's a creep, which I fucking hope I'm not." His face dips closer to mine, and he's trying to catch my eyes but I'm having a hard time looking anywhere other than his lips. "I want to show you how much I appreciate you believing in me, so can't you just let me get you dinner and walk you to your ride?"

He appreciates me? Well, you know what? I appreciate him, too. I appreciate the breadth of his shoulders, and the sexy edge of his jaw, and most of all, the way he smells so wonderfully delicious. With his hands on me, and his face so near to mine, it takes very little for me to close the distance between us and press my lips to his. I've had a lot of bad ideas in my life, and this has to be the worst. He's so wrong for me, and kissing him could jeopardize my job, but with him so intoxicatingly close, I can't bring myself to care.

His entire body stiffens. I flick my tongue out. Mm, he tastes as good as he smells. A low rumble works its way up his chest, and then he's grabbing me tightly, his hands dropping to my ass and hauling me into his body, where a very impressive ridge grinds into the V at the top of my legs. I want him closer, so I go onto my toes, letting him take most of my weight, kissing him with everything I have. It's rough and wild and out of control. I can definitely believe this is a man who hasn't been with anyone in months. His lips clash, teeth gnash, and then he's trailing open-mouthed kisses down my neck, stopping to nip at the juncture of my neck and shoulder. I gasp, and sigh, and clutch him.

"Fuck," he swears. "Lena, cutie pie, you feel so fucking good."

I rock into him, loving his ragged breaths, and the groan that rips from deep in his throat. He's big, and hot, and demanding, his hands journeying up my body and touching, squeezing, plumping my breasts, fisting in my hair and pulling my head back so he can latch onto my neck. His stubble is rough against my skin, and his teeth graze over the pulse that's throbbing furiously. Moaning, I try to yank him closer, impossibly closer.

Then a wolf-whistle pierces the air.

My befuddled mind can hardly comprehend it, but Jase shifts, shielding me from onlookers with his body. After a moment, he draws back, still panting, and wipes his mouth with the back of his hand. It's swollen from my kisses, and I imagine mine looks much the same.

"Stop looking at me like that," he growls. "It's unfair."

Seems perfectly fair to me. He's distracting me just by existing. Turnabout is fair play.

"Here's what's going to happen," he says. "I'm gonna walk you to your car, then you're going to sit your hot little ass in the driver's seat and go home. Understood?"

I nod, because he's right. That's what needs to happen, for both our sakes. Then, once I'm home, my vibrator is going up to its maximum setting, and I'll lie back and pretend we didn't do the sensible thing.

"I'm totally with you."

Chapter 15

Scene 15

Jase

My balls have never been so fucking blue in my life. My cock is hard for the entire drive home, and I have to unzip my jeans to give it a little breathing space. It's only when I'm finally alone in my bedroom that I take it in my hand and stroke. I imagine Lena's fingers wrapped around me, pumping up and down, ticking the bottom of the shaft. Pre-cum oozes from the tip and I smooth it over the head, picturing Lena dropping to her knees and taking me in her mouth. It's a tight fit, because I'm big, and despite her fiery attitude, she's a delicate woman.

"Fuck." My balls draw up tight as she swallows around me, and my hips jerk, fucking her face. I squeeze my eyes shut, back against the wall, jaw clenched. "Fuck. Lena. Baby."

I come hard, shuddering with the force of it, spilling all over my goddamn legs. I milk every last drop and flop back, breathing heavily. Minutes later, when my legs are no longer jelly, I clean myself up in the shower. But as I'm soaping, the image of taking Lena against the wall fills my mind, and though I'm raw and sensitive as fuck, I jerk off again, wishing it was her little pussy wrapped around me rather than my own coarse hand.

I remind myself of the rules. No sex before a big fight. But shit, I'd like to make an exception for her. If that dickhead hadn't wolf-whistled at us tonight, I might have dragged her into the nearest alley. And while I'd have had no problem screwing her anywhere I could, I have a feeling she wouldn't appreciate alley sex. She's classier than that. Even if she's broke.

And shit, I wasn't expecting that either.

We both misjudged each other, and though we mayhave started out on the wrong foot, I'm going to fix it.

* * *

For the first time I can remember, I'm impatient to leave the gym. I'll be seeing Lena tonight at the community center, and it's all I can think of. I'm excited the same way I was about losing my virginity, with a kind of schoolboy eagerness that's fucking embarrassing.

Fortunately, none of the guys seem to have noticed. Today is the last hard sparring session before the fight, giving me a week and a half to recover and be in top shape. In accordance with tradition, I have to face off against my brothers for one long, torturous round. Every minute, they swap out, so I'm constantly facing someone fresh while growing wearier, but I keep my hands up, stay light on my feet, and drag them to the ground at the first chance I get.

The ground is my turf. Where I'm most comfortable. And they all know it. None of them are stupid enough to give me the opportunity to take them down easily, except Devon, who's completely nuts and has a death wish. It doesn't seem to matter whether he's winning, losing, or getting his face smashed—whatever the case, he grins like a freaking maniac.

That's why he's the brother I'm most wary of. Gabe is technically proficient and cold as hell, but he's always in control of himself, whereas Devon is a loose cannon. Half the time, none of us have any clue what he's about to do, which makes his fights the most fun to watch. He's whacked in the head, in the best possible way.

Finally, Seth calls an end to the torment and my leaden legs carry me from the cage. I lower myself to the floor and catch my breath, then go through my stretching routine. As I remove my gloves, I sit through a classic Seth-style pep talk—which basically involves a grunt and a pat on the back—then I limp to the shower.

"Bro, how come you're so fired up to get out of here?" Devon asks from the adjacent stall. "Got a hot date?"

"Got class at the center tonight," I reply, running a wet cloth over my face, neck and shoulders. "Don't want to be late for the kids."

"You sure it's got nothing to do with a certain redhead?"

"Not a thing."

"Seriously, man?" He makes a sound of disappointment. "Thought you had more game than that."

"It's nearly fight week."

He sighs. "You and your stupid rule."

Tell me about it.

I finish showering, towel dry, slip on a clean set of MMA shorts and a T-shirt, grab my gloves, and head for the center. Several of the kids are already there when I arrive, and I high-five each of them in turn. There are no outcasts in my class. The kids are a rag-tag collection, aged from four to seventeen, and belong to both genders. They're white, black, Hispanic, Asian, and everything in between. They listen to me pretty well, as I knew they would, because not many people give these kids opportunities.

After ordering them to skip for five minutes and delegating responsibility to one of the older girls to lead them through a warm-up routine, I sort them into partners and remind them how to throw a jab and a cross, then get them practicing on pads. Their equipment is the best. I bought it when I first started taking lessons here and realized there was no way they could afford their own, and nor could the center. They treat the gear like it's precious, which is sweet, but also really fucking sad because few of these kids own anything of value themselves. That's part of why I started contributing to the grant. To help kids with promise but no cash make something of themselves.

I'm correcting little Carlos's form when I feel eyes on my back and know she's here. Lena. Even though I haven't seen her, the weight of her gaze is like a caress. I can sense it on my body, and I want to go to her and shove her against the wall and pick up where we left off yesterday.

Cool it, man.

I'm here for these kids, and she's here for a job. Hauling in a deep breath, I try to tune her out, knowing we'll talk later.

Chapter 16

Scene 16

Lena

Watching Jase interact with the twenty or so children in his class shouldn't get to me, but it does. They clearly adore him, and he's heart-wrenchingly patient with them, not concerned about repeating instructions a second—or even third—time. The older boys vie for his approval, while the two teenage girls both have hearts in their eyes. I don't blame them. Seeing him in action is softening my heart in a way I can't afford. It seems that Jase Rawlins is one of the decent guys. After exchanging a few words with the man who runs the center and assuring him of my good intentions, I snap photographs of Jase with the kids, making sure not to capture their faces because I promised him I'd keep their identities private.

Jase holds pads for a tiny girl who can't be more than four, and beams at her in encouragement when she hits them. Snap. That's the money shot. All I can see of the girl is a dark ponytail, but it's Jase's expression that really sells it. Zooming in on his face, I take another, and something melts deep inside me. He's making this so easy. If only he'd told me everything up front, we could have skipped a day or two of being at odds with each other. But I suppose I can understand why he clammed up. What reason did he have to trust me? Especially when I'd made my opinion of him clear from the get-go.

I'm on his side now though, and this story is writing itself in my head. I take my phone into the ladies' restroom and call one of my contacts at Sports Daily, a magazine-style website.

"Hi, Aiden," I say when he picks up.

"Hey, Lee. What's going on?"

"I need a favor, but it'll be worth your while."

He laughs, the sound rich and deep. Girls go nuts over Aiden, and I get the attraction, but I've never seen him that way myself. "Anything that comes from the golden girl of sports PR is going to be worth my while. What are we talking about here?"

"I want a premium feature. Not for tomorrow, but perhaps the next day. As soon as you can fit me in."

He whistles, and I hear him shuffling papers in the background. "Which bad boy are we going to be spotlighting?"

I love the way he assumes I've got the goods, but not his assumption that it's a bad boy. I know I've become the girl with the magic touch as far as spoiled players go, but there are other things I'd much rather be known as.

"Jase Rawlins," I tell him.

"Oh, nice." The cogs are whirring in his brain. He knows anything with Jase will be controversial right now, and controversy sells. "Keep talking."

"I'm working on a piece. It isn't finished yet, but I can have it to you tomorrow. It comes with man candy action shots, and the real winner—one of him coaching disadvantaged kids."

Aiden thinks for a moment. "I like it. Get it to me by twelve tomorrow, and the spot is yours. Provided, of course, that you come up with the publicity gold I think you will."

"Have I ever let you down, Aids?"

"Don't get cocky, Lee, there's a first time for everything."

"Kisses, bye." I hang up before he has a chance to ask me on a date, as he invariably does. He's a nice guy, but he just doesn't do it for me. And honestly, I don't think I'm his type either, which is probably why he persists in asking. He knows I'll always say no.

Heading back to the main room, I pocket my phone and claim a chair in the corner, far enough away from anyone else that no one talks to me. I grab my notebook and start bullet-pointing ideas for the article. Every now and then, I glance up to check the action, and to get my fill of Jase. A smile is permanently stamped on his face, and he's glistening with a sheen of sweat. I can't get enough of the way his muscles move as he demonstrates kicks, punches, and rolls. They're bulging and lean and fucking glorious.

When the class finishes, he waits for the kids to leave, speaking to a few of them as they pack up, then he makes his way to me, wearing a heart-stoppingly sexy grin. I flutter on the inside.

"So?" he asks, flopping into the chair beside me. "What do you think?"

"This is amazing," I reply honestly. "I can't believe you do this."

He slants a look at me. "Because I'm just a dumb jock?"

I roll my eyes and laugh. "I'm a bit judgey sometimes, sorry. If you'd had the same experiences I've had, you'd probably be the same."

He straightens, suddenly alert, his eyes narrow. His intensity sends a shiver down my spine. "Like what?"

"Nothing. Don't worry, that's not the point." I wave my notepad at him. "This is pure awesomeness and I've got a contact who can get you a feature on Sports Daily in two days' time."

The grin is back. "Seriously?"

"One hundred percent."

"And I get to check what you write first?" he confirms.

"Nothing goes in that you're not comfortable with."

He holds up a palm and I high five it, not worrying for once about how sweaty he is. "Thanks, Lena."

"No problem." I lean forward. "Seriously, it's so great what you're doing here. How did you get started?"

He glances over at the center manager. "We're getting the eyeball. Why don't you come to my office so the next group can use the room?"

I get to my feet and follow him into the hall, my eyes dropping to his firm butt as we walk. "You have an office?"

"Nah, they just let me use it while I'm here." He holds open a door and waits for me to enter. I feel his gaze on my ass as I pass by and wonder if this is payback for ogling him. "Have a seat."

"There's only one," I point out.

He paces inside and closes the door. The snick of the latch gives me all kinds of crazy ideas about what I'd like to do to him now that we finally have privacy. Not that I should. Nothing has changed from yesterday. He's still my client, and I need to keep a professional distance. But if I'm completely truthful with myself, seeing him with those kids eased my mind with regards to my other concern—the one about him being violent. Anyone who can be so gentle with a four-year-old girl is surely not a vicious person, regardless of his line of work.

"If I sit now, I'll seize up," he says. "Need to keep moving for a while."

Folding myself into the chair behind a pockmarked desk, I watch him wear a path on the floor, back and forth. "So, tell me the story."

Still pacing, he catches my eye, then breaks off the contact as he turns. "Like I told you yesterday, I grew up in foster care and moved around a lot, especially as a teenager. Fifteen-year-old boys with a chip on their shoulder aren't at the top of foster parents' wish lists."

He spins on his heel, his gaze burning into mine, and prickles of lust shoot south at the same time as my heart aches for him. How must it have felt to be cast aside? To know nobody wanted you? Even if my parents have never been what you might call traditionally loving, I never doubted they wanted me. I don't say anything, letting him continue at his own speed.

"The MMA gym one of my foster fathers ran was the first place I belonged. I had a lot of anger, and I worked it out on those mats. The guys were really accepting. I can't have been easy to get along with, but they made room for me. Even when I had to move on, I kept going back. Then, when I moved again, I found a new MMA gym."

"It sounds like MMA is important to you," I say softly.

He nods, coming over to me and drawing me to my feet. "It's my religion. The thing that gives me direction, purpose, and a sense of things being all right. That's why I started doing this. I wanted to give these kids that same experience." He swallows, the cords of his throat moving, and those gray eyes of his are hot but full of pain at the same time. "If I can do that for even one of them, then I've succeeded."

I can't believe this guy is the same one who sat opposite me in my office three days ago, giving me lip. I was blind not to see the depth he has. And while my heart thumps erratically, yearning to remove the shadows of his past, my body craves him. I want to take him in my arms and soothe his wounded soul. I want to kiss him, to smooth my hands over the planes and dips of his muscles and tug him closer. But most of all, I want him to fill the empty, throbbing part of me that wakes up every time he's around.

You can't, Lena.

Jase's hands land on my shoulders, and he brushes my hair back, his thumbs sliding over the sensitized skin of my neck. He's studying me like I'm a math problem he needs to solve, and then slowly, agonizingly, his lips claim mine and lay waste to my good intentions.

Chapter 17

Scene 17

Jase

The way Lena looks at me like she's seeing something beautiful is too damn much. I can't take it. I have to kiss her, and once I've stolen a taste, I want more. My tongue plunges deeper into her mouth and I haul her fully into my arms. She slings a leg over one of my hips, and I grab fistfuls of her butt as she wraps those legs around my waist, her skirt riding up to reveal thighs that are milky against the tan of my arms.

Fuck, she's sexy. My arms are full of warm, willing Lena. She's attacking my mouth with the same vigor I did hers a moment ago, and I can't think of anything better. I dig my fingers into the flesh of her ass and she moans, the vibrations tickling my lips.

Warning sirens are blaring in my head. I have a fight in less than two weeks, and my rule is never to fuck around at a time like this. The trouble is, whatever I'm doing with Lena—which feels damn good, by the way—isn't just fucking around. It's something real. Tonight she's made me feel good about myself in a way no other woman has, and it's got nothing to do with the number of belts I've won, or the

size of my dick. She honest-to-God cares about Jase Rawlins—the
man, rather than the champion.

Her tongue tangles with mine and she grips my shirt and jerks it,
a growl of frustration coming from the back of her throat. Despite
myself, I laugh. She sounds like a grumpy kitten, and it's the cutest
thing I've ever heard.

She swats me. Her lips are pouty, her lipstick smeared, eyes slum-
berous. "Don't laugh at me, Rawlins."

Reluctantly, I ease back and lower her to the ground. She slides
down my body, and the friction has me hard enough to hammer
nails. When I gasp, her eyes light up. She rubs herself over me again,
and I grit my teeth, breath hissing between them.

"Lena," I pant. "Slow down."

Her palms rest flat on my chest, over my heart, and hell if I don't
love the sensation. "Don't wanna."

"Look." I step back, creating a few inches of space. "There's clearly
something going on between us, but if we're going to do anything
about it, our first time shouldn't be in a crappy office with people
down the hall." Though if she keeps looking at me like that, it just
might be.

Lena licks her lips. "Fair point," she says, and although she's agree-
ing with me, my dick droops in disappointment. "Why don't we take
this to my place?"

And it perks right up again, the horny fucker. "You mean it?"

Those pouty lips fashion themselves into a smile. "Yeah, I do. I
shouldn't, but I can't seem to help myself when it comes to you."

Hell, I'm not a saint, and I'm not about to look a gift horse in the mouth. Screw the rules. I drop my shoulder and toss her over it. "Where'd you park?"

Squealing, she thumps my back. "Put me down!"

"Not gonna happen."

I pick up her purse and carry her fireman-style through the center and out to the parking lot. I took an Uber earlier because I don't like to show up in my expensive ride and flaunt my wealth in everyone's faces. I spot her ridiculous car and head toward it. Gently, I lower her onto the hood and stand between her knees, cupping her face to kiss her. She nips my lip, and I laugh.

"Guess I deserved that."

"More than that, asshole." But there's no heat in her words.

"Give me your keys."

Her lips form a mutinous line. "It's my car, so I'll drive."

I'll admit, I'm not above slipping my hand up her skirt to cup her pussy, which has soaked her underwear and radiates heat. I touch her lightly. Teasingly. Her eyes darken.

"Are you prepared to break land speed records to get there?" I ask.

She digs into her purse and hands me her keys. I unlock the driver's door and she primly tugs her skirt down and stalks around to the passenger side, shooting me glares. If I hadn't had my hand on her just seconds ago, I'd think she wanted to do me damage, but her body doesn't lie. She craves me, just as I crave her.

True to my word, I follow her directions and arrive at her apartment building in record time. I park in the basement and she leads me to an elevator, then presses the button for the third floor. While the elevator travels upward, I wrap my arms around her from behind, drawing her into the shelter of my body. Her ass curves into my eager cock, and I pepper kisses along the length of her neck. She sighs, and relaxes into me, her eyes fluttering closed.

Fuck, she's beautiful. And so freaking trusting. From here, there are so many ways I could hurt her, but she's totally at ease in my arms, and something deep in my chest squeezes. I vow, from this minute on, that I won't let anyone do wrong to this woman. I may have only known her for a few days, but somehow she's wormed her way into my soul. She's mine to protect. Mine to possess. And, if I have my way, mine to fuck. Only mine.

Finally, the elevator doors open, and I release Lena for long enough to drape my arm around her shoulders while she takes me to her apartment. She stops outside number 311 and pauses, key in the lock, then turns to look up at me.

"It's nothing fancy," she says, her expression uncharacteristically shy.

"Don't care." Mostly, I'm just charmed she invited me back to her place rather than trying to wrangle an invitation to mine. Her fingers fumble with the key, then she pushes the door open and enters, waiting for me to follow.

The apartment is small and well-kept. The door opens onto a living area with a couch at one end, a small coffee table in front, and a two-person dining table to the side. Behind the table is a kitchenette, and near the couch is a closed door that I assume leads to either her bedroom or the bathroom. She doesn't own much—the place has a spartan feel about it—but there are potted plants on the table and kitchen counter. She catches me looking at them.

"They're succulents." Her lips twist wryly. "The only thing I can keep alive."

"Except yourself," I offer.

She laughs. "True. But like I said, nothing fancy."

She seems to need reassurance, so I pull heragainst my side, bury my face in her hair, and murmur, "It's cute, just likeyou."

Chapter 18

Scene 18

L ena

At this point, my courage is fading fast. I haven't had a man in my apartment in ages. Especially not one like Jase, who could buy and sell it without even blinking, while I barely manage to make rent some weeks. I never brought Karson here. He always insisted on me visiting his place because it's literally a mansion—his favorite things are living in luxury, and showing off. But Jase doesn't seem to mind. His lips touch my forehead, and the gesture is so damn sweet I almost tear up.

"My bedroom is through here." Taking his hand, I tug him toward the door beside the sofa before I have time for second thoughts. The walls are painted cream, the bedspread is pale blue—the same color as my eyes—and I only have one set of drawers and a closet, which is packed full of the outfits and the jewelry I took when I left home.

A connecting door leads to the attached bathroom, where I store my makeup and cosmetics, but Jase doesn't need to see that, so I close it before he has time to peek. A pair of large, strong hands land on my shoulders, and his thumbs knead the tension from between my shoulder blades.

I moan. "Oh, my God. That's so good." I lean into his ministrations. "Don't stop."

"Wouldn't dream of it." His voice is husky and low, and reminds me of exactly why I invited him back here. I want this man to break my dry spell. I want the impressive erection I felt earlier sliding inside me. The sooner, the better. Before I start questioning my choices.

His clever thumbs continue working the tension from my back and shoulders, relaxing me bit by bit. He digs into a particularly tight knot and I whimper. He stiffens against me, his hands slipping, then recovers and dips his mouth near my ear.

"You make the hottest sounds."

If I didn't love the way he's touching me, I'd be mortified. Instead I push closer and brush my ass into the front of his shorts, feeling once again how much he wants me.

"If you take off your shirt, I can make you feel even better," he murmurs, his voice silky and so tempting it should be illegal.

Grabbing the hem of my blouse, I yank it over my head, then with a flick of my fingers, I dispose of my bra and present my bare back to him. Somehow, the fact I can't see him only makes it more erotic when I hear his quick intake of breath and feel the quiver of his fingers before he resumes the massage. His scent wafts over me. Deep heat and earthiness that's so masculine I can't stand it. Turning, I burrow my face into his chest, inhaling the wonderful manliness of him.

Instantly, his hands go to my tits, curving around them. Shivering, I rock into his lower body, and at the same time, whip his shirt up so I can taste the skin of his chest. He releases me and wrestles the shirt off, then gathers my breasts in his palms and drops his head to lick them. The tip of his tongue flicks my nipple, then the flat of it glides over, soothing.

"Oh. God." My knees quake. Clutching his head, I keep him there, forgetting my mission to explore his own naked chest, but that doesn't stop me from appreciating as much as I can see of it. Dark hair dusts him, enough to be noticeable, but not enough to be considered a pelt. The tattoos I've previously admired extend from his arms across his pecs, leaving a narrow strip of virgin skin down the center. In the future, I fully intend to trace the edge of his ink with my mouth. I'll never get enough of him. He's addictive as a double-whip mocha with hazelnut syrup.

His rough hands smooth down my stomach and into the waist-band of my skirt, pushing it down. I slip it off, and then I'm standing in front of him in heels, the lacy scrap of my panties, and nothing else. He eyes me greedily, exactly like a virile alpha male who's denied himself pleasure for far too long. Which, you know, he is.

"Holy fuck," he mutters, his attention snagged on my underwear. "I can't wait to tear that off and make you scream." He shakes his head. "You call those panties? That's a fucking wet dream right there."

"It's wet all right," I reply, without thinking the words through.

His slate eyes shoot to mine, and darken impossibly further. "You want me, baby?"

I nod, biting my lip to keep from sharing the details of yesterday's vibrator session with him. "Are you hard for me?"

It's a rhetorical question. The evidence is irrefutable, his shorts tented dramatically, but if I have to acknowledge my state, I want him to, too.

"So goddamned hard," he admits, stroking himself through the fabric of his shorts.

I swallow, my mouth dry. "Get naked. Now."

He strips off, and I drool a little. His thighs are bulky and strong, and his cock—wow. It's thick, really freaking long, and surprisingly well-groomed.

He takes that cock in his hand and strokes it lazily, watching me watch him. "Like what you see?"

"I'd like it more if I was touching it." Grabbing his forearm, I ease him away and smooth my fingers over the head, smearing precum down his length. He's as turned on as I am, and more than anything, I want to hear him gasp and groan and lose all of his iron willpower. As I wrap my hand around him, his entire body goes rigid, and beads of sweat roll over the ridges of his abdomen. He thrusts forward, demanding more, and I squat and lick him.

"Fuck, baby." He grabs fistfuls of my hair and jerks me forward so I take him fully into my mouth. "More."

I go to town on him, playing out many of the fantasies I've had since our first kiss, loving the way he strains and sighs and talks dirty to me. His fingers plunge into my hair, and then he's guiding me up and down the way he likes. But you know what? I want to be in control.

I pull myself off him with a pop, and his hips jerk closer, seeking me out again.

I turn my face away. "Behave yourself. This is my game."

Not willing to play by my rules, he releases his grip on my hair and jerks himself, muttering something under his breath about cock teases. I have to say, watching him pleasure himself is really working for me. I reach for him, but he draws back.

"You wanted to play silly games," he growls. "Now I'm playing. Sit on the bed and show me your pretty pussy."

My vagina purrs, pleased to have his attention. I'm eager to see where this is going, so I do as he orders, lying back and resting on my elbows, wriggling my panties off and spreading my thighs so he can see me, glistening pink and waiting for him. I dip a finger into myself and slide it through my folds, keeping my eyes on him, seeing his pupils dilate and his nostrils flare.

He takes an involuntary step forward, then seems to catch himself, and barks, "Don't touch yourself. I'm the only one allowed to touch that pussy."

I arch a brow. "Oh, really?" I don't stop, but instead slide a second finger in to join the party. "What're you going to do about it?" I don't see him move, but next thing I know he's pinned me to the bed and has my wrists above my head. A laugh escapes me. "Huh. You really are that good."

He lowers his mouth to my ear, not releasing my hands. "However good you think I am, double it. I'm the best you'll ever have, cutie pie."

I nuzzle him. "Prove it."

I expect him to thrust into me, going straight for the prize, but instead he orders me to keep my hands where they are while he slides down my body. The moment his mouth latches onto my throbbing center, my hands are in his hair. Stopping, he removes his face from between my thighs and looks at me, waiting until I return my hands above my head before continuing.

A whimper tears through me. I struggle to lie still beneath his sensual onslaught without grabbing onto something—anything—to anchor myself in the present. I can hardly believe this is actually happening. I've known this man for less than a week, and while I've had the occasional one-night stand, casual affairs aren't something I make a habit of. Especially not ones with guys like this. Men who could use me and toss me aside with a broken heart, or worse. And on top of that, ones who could jeopardize my entire career.

"Please," I gasp, needing to be on a level footing with him, needing not to come until he does, too. I can't be the weak one in this crazy whirlwind of passion. "I want you to fuck me. Right. Now."

He rises up on his elbows, and his gaze is ferocious in its intensity. "How do you like it?"

He's actually asking? It's sweet I suppose, but can't the asshole just get down to screwing me?

"Me on top." That way I retain some of the power. Based on the way he grins and buries his face in me again, he likes my answer. My head drops, my back arches up, and I'm so close—so close—but then he's gone.

I scream in frustration. But then, once I've recovered, I clamber to my knees and point a finger at him. "Bring your glorious cock back here and shove it in me, you asshole."

Giving me a wink, he holds up a condom. "Thought you might want this."

I pout. "I also wanted to come."

His cock bobs, as if it likes that answer. He sheaths himself and sits on the mattress, his back against the bed head, legs sprawled before him. "I'm at your mercy. Ride me like you want to."

And then he interlocks his fingers behind his head and leans back as though he doesn't have a care in the world. Well, I'm about to change that. Jase Rawlins will beg me for more by the time I'm done with him. While I'm not always sexually adventurous, I'm confident in myself, and in the chemistry that's been sizzling between us since day one.

Crawling up his body, I circle his dick with my fingers and lower myself onto it, just the tiniest bit. He watches, and the only thing that shows he isn't as relaxed as he'd like to appear is the way his eyes track my every movement, and his jaw tightens. When I slide him inside me another inch, his hips reflexively tilt up, and I lift off him.

Yeah, I'm as good at playing games as you.

I ease myself onto him again, until his thick head is inside me, and circle my hips. Then, before he can do anything about it, I pull away. I continue the torture, taking a little more of him each time until his abs are quivering with restraint and, finally, I'm fully seated on him. I begin to move and he snaps, losing all hint of the laid-back role he's been playing. He grips my hips and slams me down onto him. I love the slapping sound of our skin.

"Was that fun for you?" he asks. "You like driving me out of my fucking mind?"

Before I can answer, one of his arms curves around my lower back and he tugs me even closer, claiming my mouth in a kiss that's hot and carnal and wild. I'm amazed at how in sync our bodies are. When I press down, he thrusts up, and we keep pace with each other, him muttering filthy encouragements under his breath, then groaning when I mix it up and corkscrew onto him. I moan as he touches a place deep within me that I never knew existed.

"Oh, God," I cry, and he kisses my neck, licks the bottom of my earlobe, then takes it between his teeth.

"You're so beautiful," he tells me. "So amazing and fiery and god-damn perfect."

Something inside me thaws. Something I'd never planned on giving Jase Rawlins access to, and I realize, as the most wonderful sense of rightness sings in my veins, that if I'm not careful, he could steal my heart.

Then his tongue is in my mouth, and we're breathing as one, moving as one. Up and up, carrying each other higher, until blackness flickers behind my eyelids and we crash over the pinnacle of pleasure together. I hear a voice, and realize I'm chanting his name. He thrusts once more, curses, and goes limp beneath me, his arms holding me so tight I can hardly breathe.

Wow.

Now that's what it's all about. That's what it's like to be with a man who cares about mutual satisfaction. Completely spectacular.

The sweat cools on my skin, and I wonder if I should get off him. What's the etiquette after you've finished having your way with a guy like Jase? He probably doesn't want me flopping on top of him like so much dead weight. Shifting position, I try to move, but he won't let me go.

"Just another minute," he murmurs, and I submit, resting my chin awkwardly on his shoulder. A smile steals over my face. Is he catching his breath, or is the big bad MMA fighter actually snuggling me? After his allotted minute, he lets me go, and I hop off, grab my blouse and yank it over my head.

"Hold up," he says, as he disposes of the condom. "I was enjoying the view."

So. Am. I.

Although his cock is droopy, it shows signs of recovering, and he's just standing in my doorway looking like an advertisement for invisible Calvin Kleins.

"Shirt off, and back on the bed," he orders.

I consider arguing, but I'm not the type to bite off my nose to spite my face, so I whip the blouse off and lie on the bed. Jase whistles and eyes me appreciatively, then stretches alongside me. Slipping an arm beneath my waist, he draws me to his side. I rest my cheek on his chest, and it's official. We're cuddling. He threads the fingers of his free hand through mine, and turns to nuzzle the crook of my shoulder. It frightens me how much I like it. Being held by him is second only to feeling his stiff length inside me. He's such a warm person, more so than I'd ever imagined, and I'm shocked how protective I feel over him. It's laughable, considering he's physically far more capable of defending himself than I am, but who protects him from emotional harm?

Me. That's who. From now on, it's my job to keep the generous man hiding inside this tattooed, muscular exterior safe from anyone who might threaten him. But before I go announcing that to the world, I need to know I'm safe with him.

"Hey, Jase," I say tentatively. "We can just keep this between ourselves, right? It's kind of frowned upon at work to bang the clients."

He drops a tender kiss on the side of my neck. "Sure thing, baby. It's our secret."

Chapter 19

Scene 19

J ase

Two days later, I wake after a vivid dream during which I somehow coaxed five orgasms from Lena like the sex machine I am, and she rewarded me with the mother of all blow jobs. My thighs are shaking, dick spreading goo all over the sheets. Since the bedding is clearly a loss, I finish myself off with a couple of tugs, then put the sheets in the wash and have a shower. My cleaner comes a couple of times a week, but there's no way mopping up jizz is in her job description.

Once I'm clean and dry, I wrap a towel around my waist and check my phone. Then I blink in astonishment. Fifteen missed calls? The only time this has ever happened was after I dumped Erin. I check the numbers, but they're all different. Cautiously, I play the first voicemail. It's Nick.

"Jase, my man. That publicist we hired is pure gold. People have been ringing for you nonstop since her article came out last night, and ninety percent of the calls are positive. You owe her a bonus and you should also consider getting on your knees and kissing her toes. Seriously, have you read it? Give me a call."

The second message is from Devon, and it's along the same lines. Apparently, Lena is a genius and I should worship at her altar. I grin because it crosses my mind that I already have, and I wouldn't mind doing so again. Perhaps she'll have time to see me tonight. She was too busy yesterday, working on her article and then revising it after I made some suggestions.

I listen to another thirteen messages, including three invitations to hook up from women I've never met. I delete those. The only woman I want to be with right now is the one responsible for the rapid change in my fortunes. Strolling over to open the curtains and let the sun in, I dial Lena's number.

"You're fucking fantastic," I say when she answers. "Thank you, thank you, thank you."

She laughs, and I picture the cute smile that must be twisting her lips. "You're very welcome. I'm glad it's helping."

"Helping?" I shake my head. "That's an understatement. You're brilliant. I'm so grateful I could kiss you."

"Oh?" Is it just me, or did her voice drop an octave and become husky?

"Abso-fuckin-lutely."

"I'm just doing my job."

"Hell, yeah. Doing it like a boss."

She chuckles again. "Well, once you stopped being a dick, my job was surprisingly easy."

The comment doesn't bother me in the least because I was being a dick, and she was being uptight. Neither of us made the best first impression, but that's neither here nor there.

"Can I see you tonight?" I'm shocked to find my heart lodged in my throat while I await her reply. I desperately want to watch her eyes flash with passion, and see her tempting lips pout for a kiss.

"Actually..."

I'm not sure I like the way she draws the word out. "Yeah?"

"I need to see you about work, if you can spare the time. There's an opportunity I'd like to discuss with you."

"Whatever it is, I'm sure it'll be great. Come by the gym when you're free and I'll make time for you." The fact I'm prioritizing Lena over training should frighten me, but for some reason it doesn't. Maybe I'm in the stupid phase of the infatuation cycle, because even the thought of waiting a couple of hours to see her feels like forever.

"I'll see you later." She pauses, then adds, "I'm happy things are working out for you. Train hard."

Chapter 20

Scene 20

Lena

It's insane how nervous I am about seeing Jase. We haven't been together since we were together in every sense of the word. That night, I'd fallen asleep in his arms, then been roused early in the morning by a hard dick between my legs. He'd obviously been having a good dream, but he woke quickly when I started petting him, and we screwed slow and languid, him filling me from behind and holding me tight until we climaxed and drifted back to sleep.

When I woke again, he'd already left, but fresh coffee was in the pot and a bagel had been removed from the freezer, ready to be toasted. I have to admit, his making me breakfast just about wrecked my heart. It was such a sweet gesture, and not what I'd have expected after an evening of filthy sex with no promises of commitment. Karson never thought of me in the morning, and come to think of it, nor did most of my exes, which raises the question: am I attracted to men who are self-obsessed?

Ugh. I need to do some serious reflection, but for now, it's time to get my head on straight. I don't know how Jase will behave around me, especially considering I asked him not to tell anyone about us, but he wants to see me, so that's a good sign. Right?

Anyway, this is work. Strictly work. At least, for as long as it takes me to secure his agreement to attend a charitable fundraiser. Hopefully I won't have to twist his arm too hard, but I get the feeling Jase prefers to stay out of the limelight when it comes to this kind of thing. Strange because he seems so comfortable in front of an audience when he's in the cage.

After taking care of my office-based duties, I drive to Crown MMA Gym, park outside, and let myself in. Just inside the entrance, I encounter Devon Green. A massive grin spreads across his face and he yanks me into a bear hug, nearly lifting me from the ground. A squeak of shock escapes me, and he sets me back down, holding onto my shoulders until I'm steady.

"Thank you," he says, voice full of emotion. "I knew you could dig Jase's stubborn ass out of that hole he got himself into."

Touching my hair to make sure it's still in place, I return his smile. "We're only halfway out of the hole, but I think he'll pull through."

"So do I." He claps me on the back, and the force of it sends me reeling, the breath lurching out of my lungs. "Oh, my bad. Forgot you were such a delicate thing. Sorry about that."

Recovering, I glare at him. "I'm not delicate, you're just a giant."

He backs off, hands raised in peace. "Easy, Lena. That wasn't meant to be an insult."

I bristle. "Would you take 'delicate' as a compliment?"

"Well, no," he admits, running a meaty hand through short black hair. "But I'm a guy. You're a—"

"Oh. Hell. No." I'm not having this conversation. Devon Green is a Neanderthal, and that's all there is to it. "You're welcome," I tell him, then add, "But you can stop talking now before you make it worse."

"Great job, Dev." This wry comment comes from Gabe Mendoza, who appears behind him and offers me a hand. His grip is firm and warm, and far more pleasant than being crushed. "Seriously, thanks. What you're doing means a lot to us, although Jase probably won't tell you that himself."

"He has," I say, earning raised eyebrows from both of them. I look past them, into the gym. They're blocking the entrance. "And you're both welcome. Can I come in?"

"What?" Gabe asks, even as Devon recognizes the situation they've put me in and scuttles out of the way. "Oh."

Slipping my shoes off, I glance around until I see Jase bouncing on the balls of his feet in front of a speed bag, his fists nothing but blurs. I watch for a moment, enjoying the way sweat gleams on his skin and his muscles flex and bulge as his powerful arms move. Eventually, a timer blares and he steps away and mops his face on a towel. When he turns, our eyes catch, and a flutter-volcano erupts in my soul.

Immediately, he drops the towel and beelines toward me, greeting me with a lopsided grin. "Hey, cutie pie."

Gabe stares at him, and Devon snorts with laughter, but Jase ignores them, looping his arms around my waist and drawing me in for a thoroughly sensual kiss. The moment our lips touch, all my promises about being professional go out the window and I clutch him closer, only mildly aware of the fact his sweat is rubbing off all over me—and so is something else. Some kind of oil that reeks of menthol and is hot but icy at the same time.

"Whoa," one of the men mutters as the kiss drags on.

I plant my hands on Jase's shoulders and gently push. "What happened to keeping it quiet?"

"Oh, shit. Sorry." His face falls. "I was excited to see you." He glances at his friends. "You didn't see anything, right?"

Devon nods. "Riiight, bro. 'Course not."

"Please guys," I say. "Don't mention this."

"Don't worry. We won't," Gabe assures me, and his sincerity calms me somewhat.

"Thank you." I turn to Jase. "Can we talk in private?"

Devon guffaws. "I think that's code, bro."

Cue eye roll. "It is not. Strictly business."

Devon's eyes widen, and so does his grin. "Are you sure you wouldn't rather date me, Lena? Because I guarantee I've got more moves than this idiot." He shoves Jase playfully.

"Go away," Jase says, making a shooing motion. "I have PR stuff to do." Taking my hand, he leads me to what appears to be a changing room, where he backs me into the wall and cradles my face in his palms. "Are you sure you're really here for work?" he asks. "'Cause I think I could change your mind."

Laughing, I disentangle myself from him and circle around so he's the one with his back to the wall. "You could try. But let's be serious." I rub my lips together to moisten them because I'm not sure how he's going to react to this. "This morning the Albright Literacy Foundation reached out to me. They have a fundraiser and their keynote speaker dropped out yesterday. They saw the article about you, remembered that you're one of their big contributors, and contacted me to find out if you'd consider speaking for them. It's on Sunday."

His jaw drops almost comically. "As in, two days away? That Sunday?"

"Yeah." I swallow. "That Sunday." I grab for his hand to prevent him from escaping. "Please think about it. This is big. It could blow the article out of the water. If you do this, I promise your problems with Erin will be the last thing anyone is talking about."

He stills, then levers his jaw closed. "Will there be any other publicity stunts coming my way if I agree to this?"

"I can't say for sure, but I doubt it. This should be enough to get you back on track—unless, of course, Erin decides to press charges. But she'd need some kind of evidence in order for that to happen, and she might just decide to slink back out of sight."

He appears to weigh my words. Finally, he exhales, his big shoulders dropping. "I'm not much of a public speaker."

My lips twitch up, but I drag them down, not wanting him to see my amusement. "I'd disagree. You always know exactly what to say to build up an audience or smack talk an opponent for the cameras."

He shrugs and looks away, apparently uncomfortable with my assessment. "That's all for show, and it's all about fighting. It's not anything that really matters the way this would." He tries to turn, but I hold firm, refusing to let him hide from me. "I mean, what do I have to say that a literary crowd is going to want to hear?"

I frown. He's underestimating himself, and this lack of confidence isn't at all like the Jase I've come accustomed to. "Well..." I say, drawing the word out, searching for something to bring him around. "Why do you donate to them?"

Leaning against the wall, he gazes down at me. "Because I want to help kids get out of shit situations. For some, sports might be the way to do that, like they were for me, but for others, like Gabe's best friend Sydney, their brains are the way out."

I melt inside. How is it possible for this man to be so irresistible? So good to the core and sexy as hell at the same time. "Then talk about that. Tell them about your own situation and how you want to help others like you. Perhaps use Gabe's friend as an example, if she doesn't mind. Or instead of getting into anything specific, you could talk about how you want those kids to have options and hope for the future, and use that to fire the donators up and open their pockets." Swaying closer to him, I hold his hand between both of mine. "The whole point of the event is to get people with deep pockets to open them, so you say whatever you think will make the money flow."

Those dark gray eyes don't move from mine, and a shiver courses through me. He watches me with such intense focus that I feel like an exhibit in an art gallery.

"What if I make a dick of myself?"

The words are low, and I have to strain to hear them.

"You won't." Of that, I'm sure. He may not be the most eloquent guy, but there's something about him that's captivating. He has charisma, and any audience will sense it.

He shifts, peeling himself from the wall and encapsulating me within his arms, his hands resting on my lower back. My belly flips and fizzles, loving his nearness.

"I'll do it," he says, easing one hand down to cup my butt, "on one condition."

I nibble my lip, knowing I'll have to reapply lipstick before I leave. "What's that?"

God, could I sound any more like I want to jump his bones?

"You come with me."

"I'm sorry, what?" I'd been expecting something dirty. Hoping for something dirty. It takes me a moment to process what he's actually said.

"Be my date, Lena."

His face is hidden from me in this position, so I hear the words drift past my ear but can't see his expression as he utters them. More than anything, I want to know what the invitation means. Does he just want moral support, or is he is declaring his intention to date me publicly? Because didn't we just talk about that? Or perhaps he wants to show me that public relations isn't all fun and games. Give me a taste of my own medicine, so to speak.

I swallow. "I'm a behind the scenes person. I'm the one who talks to you through your headset to make sure you don't say the wrong thing to the wrong person. I'm not the type of person who actually goes to these events." Although I had been, once, when Karson used to drag me around like his freaking eye candy, so dolled up you wouldn't recognize me if you saw me on the street the next day. I missed so many red flags with that guy.

"You should be," Jase says, breaking into my thoughts. "You deserve to be up front and center as much as anyone else."

"Doesn't matter," I tell him as he draws back to look me in the face. "I don't enjoy being the subject of attention, and I also don't want to get into trouble with my boss."

A smile quirks his lips. "Guess what, sweetheart? I don't like the attention either. It's just the price I pay for doing what I love." He kisses me. "That's my deal. You as my date, or I don't go. You can tell your boss I'm forcing you into it. What do you say?"

"Fine," I grumble, and he captures my mouth in another kiss. Adrian is going to shit a brick when he finds out. But hopefully he'll go along with it and once Jase is out of hot water, I can work with some of those other clients he promised me. Reluctantly, I ease away from him. "I need to get back to work."

He sighs, the sound full of regret. "You mean you have clients other than me?"

"Yes, gorgeous, I do."

He lets me go, but doesn't move, so it's up to me to put distance between us. "I hope they're not as charming."

I laugh, delighted by the flash of jealousy in his gaze and how put-out he seems. "Charming, my ass. You're hot, I'll give you that."

He growls, claiming my hand and walking me toward the exit. "What else?"

"What? Does your ego need stroking?" My tone is teasing, and I enjoy the way he smiles down at me with laughter in his eyes.

"I can think of some other things you could stroke."

I smooth a hand down his arm. "Whatever."

He accompanies me all the way to my car, then backs me against it the same way he did against the wall inside. My hips roll into his, just once, then they still.

He notices though, his breath hitching. "Can I see you later?"

"Only if you're not worried about messing up your mojo." I know how superstitious athletes can be, and I truly don't want him off his game. In fact, I'd quite happily watch Jase mop the floor with Karson's face.

"Think it's more likely to mess with my mojo if my balls shrivel up and fall off," he says wryly. "You got me turned inside out, cutie pie."

Stretching up, I kiss him. "I'll see you later, then." My smile turns sly and naughty. "But not too late. I might have to get started without you."

His eyelids flutter closed. "You're going to kill me, baby. I've gotta go bust some heads. Save your first orgasm for me." He touches my neck lightly, then strides away. I watch his fine ass go, wishing I didn't have those other clients who need me.

It's going to be a long day.

Chapter 21

Scene 21

L ena
   I have to say, the whole post-sex snuggling thing is growing on me. I have no idea how a guy who's all flat planes and hard angles manages to be so wonderfully cuddly, but he is. He's like my own sexy teddy bear. My own naked sexy teddy bear, whose cock is rapidly hardening against my butt. Just as I'm about to roll over and see if he's up for more, my phone rings.

Jase's arms tighten around me. "Ignore it."

I hesitate. I'd love to, but it could be work. When I grab it, the caller ID reads: Work Wife.

"Hey, Bree," I answer, raising it to my ear.

"Hi, girl!" she exclaims, almost drowned out by traffic in the background. "I have the best news."

Heart hammering, I sit up. "Oh, yeah? What's that?"

Bree pauses to talk to someone else, and I wait for her to return. "I'm telling you this because you're kickass at your job and I want good things for you, but it goes against my instincts, because I don't want to be trapped in that hellhole alone every day."

"What is it, Bree?" I demand. "I have a naked man in my bed, giving me sex eyes."

I know her so well I can picture the exact way her lips form an 'O'. Jase waggles his brows, and mouths, "Who is it?"

"Who?" Bree asks breathlessly. "Ohmygod, tell me he's hot."

"Yeah, he's hot." I wink at Jase. "Tell you more tomorrow. How about you explain why you called?"

"I want to know more now," she complains. "You're the worst girlfriend ever."

"I'll tell you tomorrow," I repeat. "Bree..."

"Yeah, yeah." She sighs, and some of the noise behind her fades away. "You didn't hear this from me, but Englewood is hiring."

Excitement floods my veins and I clutch the phone tighter. Englewood is the public relations firm run by my idol, Maria Englewood. I listened to her speak at a conference once, and she blew my mind.

"Seriously?"

"I wouldn't lie to you, Lee. You need to apply for that job."

"You think I have a chance?"

Jase jackknifes up, a frown furrowing his forehead. When I wave away his concern, he sets his lips on the side of my neck and sucks. I can't help the little moan that escapes.

Bree shrieks with laughter, so loudly I have to hold the phone away from my ear. "You're getting it on with him right now, aren't you? Dirty girl."

"No," I protest, but that only encourages Jase, who flicks his tongue over my skin and hums like I'm the best thing he's ever tasted.

"You so are. I'm going to make this quick. Yes, you have a chance. You're as good as anyone else. Now go get some, and then submit your application."

"I will, thanks, Bree."

Jase takes the phone from me, ends the call, and tosses it aside. "What was that about?"

Before I can answer, he slides a hand down my belly and cups my sex, pressing in the most delicious way.

My head falls back onto his shoulder. "Doesn't matter."

"It does to me," he murmurs, but slips a finger into the wetness that's already forming between my thighs. "What's going on, cutie pie?"

My hips buck, and I ride his hand. "I can't think when you're doing that."

He stops, and I growl in frustration. "Talk to me."

"Fine." Sensing he's not going to get busy with me until he's heard what Bree had to say, I turn to face him and pull the sheet between us to separate my horny body from his. "That was a friend of mine from work. She was telling me about a job she thinks I should apply for."

His brow quirks up. "You don't like the job you have?"

I bide my time in replying, not wanting him to take this the wrong way. "Most of my job involves covering for spoiled jocks who think they can get away with anything, and that's not where my heart is. No offense."

His jaw clenches, like my words hurt him, but he gives a jerky nod. "What would you rather be doing?"

Rolling onto my side, I drag the sheet with me, and he does the same, propping himself up on his elbow.

"I want to work with women who have been unfairly sidelined, or people who are underprivileged. Someone for whom I could really make a difference."

He watches me with those unreadable eyes. "I think that's a really fucking cool dream. Is that what you'd be doing at this other job?"

"Maybe. The woman who runs it is amazing. I'd happily worship the ground she walks on, but..." I gnaw on my lower lip until he smooths a thumb over it.

"But what?"

"It's not a sure thing, and my manager, Adrian, promised I could have my choice of clients if I worked a miracle with you."

A teasing smile lights his face. "So you're using me for your career?"

"About as much as you're using me. The point is, I don't know if Englewood—that's the name of the firm—would even want me. If they did, there's every possibility I'd start at the bottom, doing similar work to when I started. I've already paid my dues at my current job, so maybe I should just suck it up and wait for it to finally pay off."

"Why wouldn't they want you?" Jase asks. When I laugh, he adds, "I'm serious. I've seen firsthand how good you are. They'd be stupid not to hire you. Anyway, so what if they didn't? It doesn't hurt to get in the ring and fight for what you want."

At this, I can't help but smile. Trust him to use an MMA metaphor. But he's right. The worst Englewood can do is reject me, and if Adrian knows I'm considering moving on, won't it increase my value to him?

"You know what? I think I will apply." I wriggle closer and kiss him. "Thank you for talking it through with me."

"No problem." He tears the sheet aside. "Now I'd like to claim my reward."

Slowly and deliberately, I trace my tongue around the outside of my lips. "I think that can be arranged."

He groans. Then I trail open-mouthed kisses all the way down his gorgeous body to his impressive erection, and take it in my mouth. Before long, he's groaning a whole lot more.

Chapter 22

Scene 22

J ase

My palms are sweaty as I pace the length of the living room floor, back and forth over the soft carpet, earning the occasional reproachful glance from Nick, who's seated on the sofa with his laptop on his knee, looking like he was born to wear a suit. In contrast, I feel like a gorilla stuffed into a kid's tuxedo. It's stiff and itchy and sits funny across my chest. Or maybe that's the nerves. Public speaking isn't really my thing.

But the speech I'm due to give in a little over an hour isn't the only reason I'm wound tighter than a spinning back fist. Tonight will be the first time Lena has seen my home. I usually visit hers, which we both seem to prefer. I like knowing that she isn't after me for my money or mansion, and she likes knowing I don't look down on her living situation. Damned if I know why she'd expect me to, but perhaps a douchebag ex has.

"Calm down, Jase," Nick says, looking up from his laptop. "You'll be fine. We've gone over your speech, and you know what you're doing. It'll be over soon."

"Not soon enough," I grumble, and check my phone again. No texts or calls from Lena. "We need to go. Where is she?"

Nick chuckles. "We don't have to leave for another fifteen minutes, and she's the one who arranged this, so she won't be late."

I wish I had as much confidence as he does. This niggling little fear is working its way under my skin, leaving me with a crawling dread that she'll change her mind and decide not to come. That she'll abandon me when I need her support.

Swearing, I tug at the collar of my shirt. It's insane how insecure this event is making me. Normally, I wouldn't care if a girl I was seeing bothered to turn up. I might even prefer to go alone. But right now, I crave the sound of Lena's voice telling me I'll kill it, and the sensation of her palms on my chest, over my heart. Fuck, I'm becoming a sap, and I don't even care. I'll hand over my balls for her safekeeping if it means she gets here in the next five minutes and talks me off the ledge.

I throw a jab-straight combo, shadowboxing to take the edge off my nerves. Nick sighs and props his feet up to make sure he's out of my way. Then, finally, there's a knock at the door. I hurry to answer, not caring if I seem desperate, or anxious for reassurance. I fucking am.

Throwing the door open, I start to say hello and nearly have a heart attack. My hand goes to my chest, and I swear to God, I growl. I've never made a sound like it before, but the sight of Lena in a black and red dress that reveals way too much of the most tempting tits on the planet robs me of my ability to speak. I stare at her like an asshole, and the only thing missing is the drool hanging from the corner of my mouth. I'm torn between the desire to crow my victory to anyone who'll listen, show her off and treat her like the queen she is, and the violent impulse to wrap my body around her so no other man can get an eyeful of what's rightfully mine. She has my insides twisted in so many knots I don't know if I'll be able to untie them.

What would she do if I threw her over my shoulder and dragged her to the bedroom? I want to strip her bare and see what she has beneath that dress. Is she wearing a bra? Because it doesn't look like it, and damned if I don't want to check to see if she's going commando as well. My gaze skims down her body, stopping on her toes, which have a freshly applied layer of scarlet paint and are clad in a pair of three-inch fuck-me heels. My heart stutters. She's going to be the end of me.

She clears her throat, and I rip my eyes away from her feet, feeling like a weirdo in ten different ways. Fortunately, she's smiling. Her lips are the same brilliant red as her dress, toes, and shoes. I want to lay siege to them. As far as I'm concerned, that mouth belongs to me. If that makes me a caveman, so be it.

"That's exactly what I was going for," she says, stepping closer and cocking her head. She smells like flowers, and it hits me that I should have bought her a bouquet or something. Man, I'm out of practice.

"You look fucking amazing," I tell her, laying my palms on her shoulders carefully, because she's so soft and my hands are rough. I don't want to mark her beautiful skin before we leave. "Every guy there is going to wish they were me tonight."

She smooths her hands over my chest, and I wonder if she can feel my heart thundering through the jacket. "And every woman is going to wish they were me." Her teeth catch her lower lip, scraping through the lipstick. I can't take my eyes off them. "It's not fair how good you look. Aren't fighters supposed to have cauliflower ears and crooked noses?"

"Not all of us." Although, as she knows, I have my share of scars and flaws.

"I love the way you're looking me at," she whispers. "Like you want to eat me up. But we should probably go inside and get ready to leave."

"Later?"

"Yeah." She worries her lip again and watches me with those big, gorgeous eyes. "Later."

She tries to move past me, but I hold her tight. I need to have a taste. Just one, then we'll do the responsible thing. I take her mouth with all of the savage desire that's been growing within me since I first opened the door. With a sigh of surrender, she softens against me and parts her lips. My tongue plunges in, finesse long gone, and I consume her like I'm starving. In contrast, she's gentle and relenting, letting me take what I want, giving me what I need, her whimpers muffled by my greedy kiss.

Chest heaving, I draw back. Her lips are plumper than before, the lipstick gone and natural color shining through. Groaning, I kiss her once more, softly, then back away from her.

"Sorry. Couldn't resist. You just..." I make a helpless sound, and she nods.

"I get it."

Thank God one of us does, because I don't. I've always had a healthy libido, but I've never been so overwhelmed by need for a particular woman. My cock is straining against my pants, desperate to bury itself in her, but we both pretend it's not there and eventually it begins to behave.

"Come in. Nick is already here."

She moves past me, then whips out a pocket mirror and reapplies lipstick before we continue to the living room. Why that disappoints me, I don't know. Perhaps I wanted my manager to know exactly what we were doing. As far as Lena goes, I want everyone to know what's between us, even if I don't fully understand it myself yet. Unfortunately, that's not in the cards just yet. She's determined to keep us quiet until I'm not her client anymore, and I respect that decision.

"Hi, Nick." Lena greets him with a handshake, then perches primly on the edge of an oversized armchair. Most of my furniture is super-size, because otherwise my brothers and I wouldn't be comfortable. We make them look normal, but the chair dwarfs Lena. She meets my eyes. "Do you have your speech ready?"

I nod.

"He's been practicing," Nick says. "He's ready to go, even if he doesn't believe it himself."

Her expression softens, and I become a gooey marshmallow on the inside.

"You'll be great." She touches her hair, which is arranged in ringlets over her shoulders. "You've got this, Jase. I have absolute faith in you."

Okay, so that makes me feel ten feet tall. "Thanks." My voice is gruff. I'm not comfortable talking about shit like this, but I appreciate her words more than she'll ever know. When was the last time someone else told me they believed in me? I search my mind, but I'm not sure that anyone ever has—apart from Seth, perhaps. Not a woman, certainly. "That means a lot."

And it makes me want to screw her senseless. When this fundraiser ends, Lena LaFontaine is getting really lucky.

She shrugs. "It's just the truth. Shall we get going then?"

"Guess so." There's no one else holding us up. Although I must say, she's worth every agonizing minute of the wait. With more nerves churning in my stomach than I've ever had before a fight, I take Lena's hand and tuck it into my elbow, holding her close. We head out to the driveway, where a limo is waiting, and I help her into the backseat, then climb in after her. Nick sits opposite. He's left his laptop behind but pulls a phone from his pocket and starts typing. I swear, the guy is permanently glued to technology. I bet he's even found a way to channel his sleepwaves into productive communication.

I mentally run through my speech again. I feel like such a goddamned fraud to be speaking at an event about literacy when I can't remember the last time I read anything that wasn't on social media, but Lena's presence steadies me. She wouldn't have signed me up for this if she didn't believe I could do it. Reaching over, I take her by the waist and lift her onto my lap.

"Stop manhandling me in front of your manager," she mutters, leaning close so Nick can't hear. Not that he'd notice if she yelled it out of the sunroof. He's absorbed in whatever is on his phone.

"You don't really want me to stop," I reply, more confident than I actually am.

Sighing dramatically, she settles into my lap and loops one of her arms around my neck. "Okay, maybe not. But don't mess with my hair, or we're going to have a problem."

"Wouldn't dream of it." Although I'm having fantasies about tugging on those curls while she rides me. My dick stirs again. She raises an eyebrow. What can I say? I'm a horny bastard where she's concerned.

I keep her on my lap until we arrive at the fundraiser, where Nick pockets his phone and waits for me to leave the limo first. Apparently I'm expected to make a big entrance. I take Lena's arm, bringing her along with me, so when I step into the flashing lights of a dozen cameras, she's by my side. We cross a paved pavilion and walk up a staircase lined with reporters and photographers. None of them can get close to me, which means this is my jam. I can handle public displays just fine from a distance. It's when they want me to talk that my confidence plunges.

Lifting a hand, I wave to a guy I recognize from one of the big sports channels, and nod to a popular YouTuber who once did a flattering feature on me. They're rabidly curious about Lena, I can see it from here, and she must be able to as well because she flattens herself to me as though she's trying to make herself small and inconspicuous. Fuck that, she looks like a million bucks and she deserves to know it.

"Guess what?" she murmurs as we reach the top. "There's a big difference between knowing thirty different media outlets will be present and being on the receiving end of all that attention."

Planting my hand in the small of her back, I simultaneously guide her inside and stake a claim on her in case any of the other assholes here decide to look her way. "Welcome to stardom."

She makes a noise that could be a laugh, but sounds more like a squeak from a terrified rabbit. "I prefer being on the other side of the rope."

Pausing, I press a kiss to her temple, ignoring the buzz below. "Thank you for coming. You're doing great." Strangely enough, helping her cope with her nerves eases mine. "Let's find our table."

Unfortunately, as soon as we enter, someone whisks me away from Lena and I glance over my shoulder to see her wide eyes disappear into a sea of faces. I'm taken to a back room where a guy in a designer suit barks instructions, and next thing I know a half hour has passed and I'm being ushered onto a stage, in front of more than fifty tables full of people. They all have their faces turned toward me.

I swallow, then clear my throat. "Good evening, everyone." My voice is too loud in the sudden silence, and sweat breaks out on my upper lip. What am I doing here? Who am I kidding? This isn't the place for me. I check the notes I wrote on my palm earlier, but the ink has smudged because my damn palms are sweating, too.

"It's great to be here," I say, improvising. The tie is too tight around my neck and I'm not sure I can breathe. But then I catch sight of a brilliant black and red dress, and a beautiful head of curls, and the pressure on my throat eases. Lena smiles at me, and nods. I nod back, and stand straighter. I've got this. Lena believes in me, and I'm all over this speech. I've said it a dozen times over the last few hours. So I open my mouth and let the words fall out. Lena's grin widens, and I talk directly to her. People laugh and applaud, but I don't hear them because all of my focus is on my girl.

When I come to the end of my speech, someone claps me on the shoulder and my gaze tears away from hers. I reel back, feeling like I've stumbled out of a pleasant daydream. The audience are standing, and for the life of me, I can't even remember what I said. But I smile and step back, seeking Lena out again. She's looking away, talking to Nick, but she's beaming and I'm so fucking pleased to be responsible for that expression.

The MC takes over, and I'm excused. All of my instincts scream at me to run to Lena's table and kiss the hell out of her, but instead I find an empty room, shut myself inside and close my eyes. In my mind, I can still see her as clearly as if she's right in front of me, and it fills me with warmth.

I'm in trouble. Because not only am I crazyattracted to Lena and more than a little possessive of her, but I think I'mfalling for her, too. And that isn't okay. I don't have time for a girlfriend.Not one who deserves a man who'll conquer the world for her. But fuck, I wish I did because everything about her feels right, and I want her with me forever.

Chapter 23

Scene 23

L ena

I'm so proud of Jase. I know how nervous he was, but the crowd loved him. It doesn't hurt that he's easily the sexiest guy here, with his broad shoulders, smoldering eyes, and confident swagger.

"Hey, Lena, is that you?"

Glancing over my shoulder, I spot Travis, a linebacker for the new Vegas football team, who's also a former client of mine. Another former client, hockey star Brent Wallace, is standing beside him, both of them with drinks in hand. We're free to mingle until the dinner service, and Travis has a glint in his eye that says he wouldn't mind mingling with me in ways I'd rather not think about. He heads toward me, people scattering in his wake, and brings Brent with him.

I scan the room, but there's no way I can dodge them, so I resign myself to brushing off Travis's lame-ass pickup lines. In a lot of ways, he isn't a bad guy. There are many worse. But he's spoiled, self-centered, and never learned to take "no" for an answer. Especially where women are concerned.

"Nice to see you, gorgeous," he says, ducking to kiss my cheek, where he lingers long enough for me to grow uncomfortable. He gives me a once over, pausing on my chest. "You look great, as always. Do you know my buddy Brent?"

"Yes." I offer a hand to Brent, who shakes it. He's quieter than Travis, more the brooding type, and while he's easier to deal with, he unsettles me. "Good to see you."

"What are you doing here?" Travis asks, crowding closer. "Brent, why don't you get her a drink?"

I shake my head. "I'm fine, thanks." I'm not drinking anything either of these two give me. Not that I necessarily think they'd slip me something, I just don't fully trust them. They're accustomed to doing whatever they want, and having someone else clean up their mess. Someone like me.

"So, why are you here?" Travis persists, sipping his wine. "Did you decide you want in on some of the action yourself?"

"Hardly." I laugh. "You know this isn't my scene." I don't want to reveal too much personal information to them, but I'm getting the impression I should dissuade Travis's interest as quickly as possible. "I'm here with someone."

"With someone." He tests the words, as though they're unfamiliar. "Like a date?"

"No. Yes." I sigh. "He's a client."

If anything, the interest in his eyes intensifies. "I thought you liked to keep your personal life separate from work."

Generally, I do, so I can't argue the point. But then an arm is circling my waist and I'm being pulled into the shelter of a male body.

"Cutie pie." A masculine voice rumbles beside my ear, and I shiver. Jase. Thank God. "Introduce me to your friends."

Turning in his arms, my hands go to his chest. His jaw is tight, eyes narrowed on the two men across from me, who are staring, rapt. Smoothing a hand on Jase's cheek, I redirect his face down to me. Immediately, his jaw loosens and he smiles.

"You were great up there," I tell him, and after glancing around to make sure no one has a camera aimed our way, I stretch onto my tiptoes for a kiss. I only intend for it to be a brief touching of lips, but he secures me against him and ravages me so thoroughly I know I'll need to fix my lipstick. When he pulls away, there's a smear of red in the corner of his mouth and I wipe it off with my thumb. I want to be annoyed at him for kissing me like that in full view of everyone, but it's hard to be mad when my body is zinging with attraction and my hormones are going crazy.

"Thanks, baby." He turns back to Travis and Brent, wearing a cocky, challenging grin. "Sorry, remind me what your names are?"

To my utter surprise, Travis sticks his hand out, eyes wide with hero worship. "Travis McMillan, pro football player. It's such an honor to meet you. I saw your fight against Jarrod Hamilton live. So. Fucking. Savage."

Some of the tension fades from Jase's body, and I stop worrying he's about to grab one of them in a stranglehold and undo all of the good we've accomplished tonight. "Always nice to meet a fan. You ever fought?"

"Nah." Travis shakes his head. "I've considered it, but football is more my speed. Doesn't mean I don't love watching though. How are you feeling about the championship bout next week?"

Jase shrugs. "Can't spill my secrets ahead of time." He jerks his chin at Brent. "How about you? What's your story?"

Brent grabs Jase's hand a little too eagerly. "Brent Wallace. I play for the Golden Knights in the NHL."

"Huh. A hockey man." The way he says this, it's impossible to tell if he's impressed or not. "What position?"

"Defense."

"Nice."

Travis glances my way, expression incredulous. "You're dating Jase Rawlins?"

"Yeah." There's no point lying now, although I feel like I should be insulted by his incredulity. "It's just new."

"But it's good," Jase adds, pulling me closer. His hand, now free from the manly shaking, settles on my hip in a way no one could mistake for friendly. I manage not to roll my eyes, but it's obvious he's marking his territory. Frankly, it's a little ridiculous. The moment he appeared, neither of the men could have been less interested in me.

Brent leans in, his expression something other than blank for once. "How did it feel to fight Rory MacIlraith?"

Jase replies, but I don't hear him because I've zeroed in on the man approaching from behind Travis and Brent. My blood turns icy, and

I dig my fingernails into my palm. I'd happily never see that man ever again, but he walks steadily toward us, his dark blond hair brushed back from his face, emphasizing sharp cheekbones and a cleft chin. People hurry to get out of his way. No one wants to get between Killer Karson Hayes and his destination, which appears to be me. And that's when I notice the woman at his side. Jase's ex, Erin. Well, fuck. That can't be good. Especially since I haven't come clean with Jase about who my ex is or why I ended things. I break out in a cold sweat.

"Rawlins."

My jaw locks in place. I can't open it. Can't speak. Karson has this way of talking as though everyone is beneath him. It's a bored, condescending drawl.

Asshole.

Jase meets his eyes, and the guys he's been speaking to step aside, watching excitedly, like they expect a brawl to break out right in front of them.

"Hayes," Jase replies with a nod. I've always thought the way men do that is stupid. What's the point of it? His gaze lowers to Erin, who is dressed spectacularly, in a short black dress and stunning heels. She leans into Karson, looking like the gold-digger I suspect she is.

Girl, you don't know what you've gotten yourself into.

Even though I don't like Erin, I want to warn her that Karson is bad news. No one deserves to be on the receiving end of his shitty behavior. But I can't exactly say that right now.

"Erin," Jase continues, his tone chilling further. "You're a piece of work."

Erin doesn't reply—she doesn't have the chance because Karson gets there first. "I see you're enjoying my cast-offs." Vengefulness glimmers in his shark-like eyes. "You look fresh from the trailer park, Lena." His brow quirks. "Have I seen that dress before?"

Oh man, I'm in for it now. I wish like hell the floor would dissolve beneath me so I don't have to hear what's coming.

He cocks his head, relishing my obvious horror. "In fact, I think I bought it."

Yeah, there it is. He shoots, he scores. Jase stiffens beside me, but he doesn't give away his shock—a fact I appreciate immensely. But then I notice his hands are fisted, and he's poised and ready to pounce. Oh, shit. He's not going to get into a fight on my account, is he? Pain throbs behind my temples. No, no, no.

"I traded up," Jase says, stroking a hand over my hip like he's trying to reassure me. I don't find his expression reassuring in the least. "From where I'm standing, it looks like you traded down." He gestures at Erin. "You've got to watch that one. She'll have a knife in your back the minute you turn it."

Karson bares his teeth in a frightening grin. The one I see in my nightmares. "I like girls with a little fight in them. Makes it even hotter when they break."

I try not to cower. I try so damn hard. But he gives me a cold, calculating look. He knows he's getting to me, and he likes it. Fucker. Jase must sense it too, because the hand that's been stroking me stills, and he curves his body around mine, shielding me from my ex. I turn into him, and he gently touches my chin, raising my eyes to his. They're soft and concerned, but there's fire flickering behind them. He's angry.

No, he's furious.

"You want to get out of here, cutie pie?" he asks.

"Yes, please."

My voice is a quiet rasp, but he hears me and looks over at Karson. "We've got better places to be," he says. "See you in the cage, loser."

And then he's whisking me from the room, out the side exit to avoid cameras. When we're on the sidewalk, I just stand there and shiver while he summons a taxi, then drapes his jacket over me.

"What do you need?" he asks.

I blink up at him, determined not to cry. "Ineed you. Can we just be together?"

Chapter 24

Scene 24

Jase

Holy fuck. The guy I'm about to battle for the championship belt is Lena's ex? In what universe does that make sense? And why didn't she tell me?

She said he'd been involved in MMA, but there's a difference between "involved" and "my biggest rival." The guy is a Grade A douche. All fighters talk a lot of shit, but most don't mean it. He does, one hundred percent. Karson has a mean streak. Likes to make people bleed and give them the kind of injuries they can't walk away from. I may be a nasty fucker to face off against, but I don't aim to ruin people's careers. I just give the audience what they want so I get paid.

Lena is bundled up beside me in the back seat of the taxi. The driver is taking us to my place because it's closer. She won't look at me, and she's hugging her knees to her chest. Does she think I'm mad? Because I'm not. Just confused.

"Lena."

She nods, but doesn't glance my way.

"You used to date Karson?"

She nods again, then clears her throat. "Yeah."

An answer. That's something. "Was it serious?"

She continues to stare forward. We're not far from my house now, and I'm eager to get her somewhere she feels more comfortable.

"We were together for about three months."

I lay my hand over hers, dying for a peek of her pretty eyes so I can see what's going on in her head, but I can't, so I ask what I really want to know. "What happened?"

Finally, her eyes meet mine, and the misery in them hits me like a knee to the kidneys. "I ended it with him because he..." Pressing her lips together, she seems to shore up her courage. I hate seeing her like this when she's usually so sassy and full of life. "He hit me, and I wasn't okay with that."

Fuck. No.

My temper flares, and my blood pressure skyrockets. I can't see anything but Lena. The edges of my vision are fogged with red.

I'll kill him. I'll fucking kill the bastard, and I won't regret it for a second.

"He's a dead man." Adrenaline rushes to my muscles and I want nothing more than to punch or kick something. To take someone down. But I can't. Not here. And that kind of reaction isn't what Lena needs, so I struggle to contain it. "I should have planted my fist in his face instead of walking away." Guilt washes over me. My girl needed defending, and I didn't do it.

"No, Jase." She releases her knees and takes my hand, having recovered enough to give me her whole attention. Even better, the fire is back in her eyes, along with a dose of blood lust. "I'm glad you didn't. I've worked hard to get you out of trouble. But"—she moistens her lips with her tongue—"I want you to crush him."

That, I can do. I've trained harder for this fight than any other, and after hearing her story, I'm either leaving the cage victorious, or he'll have to knock me the fuck out. Nothing short of that will stop me from kicking his puny ass.

"Consider it done. You want me to break any bones while I'm at it?"

Her lips quirk up. I'm getting through to her. She's not shivering as much as she was, and she's starting to lean into me.

"Maybe his nose," she replies. "The uglier you can make it, the better."

"I'll make him so ugly, he never gets laid again."

She laughs, and I rejoice. Then the taxi pulls up, and I pay the driver and help Lena from the cab.

"How do you feel about hot tubs?" I ask, steering her with a hand on the small of her back. "'Cause I'm seeing one in your future."

"I love hot tubs." She grins over at me, and the strain of our encounter with Karson seems to have worn off. "Please tell me you have one with jets."

"I do. It's important for loosening my muscles after a hard training session. I have a sauna, too." Personally, I don't love the sauna. I have too many memories of sitting inside hot boxes trying to sweat off weight to make the grade for a fight. But Lena sighs happily and rests her head on my shoulder as I unlock the door. When we're inside, I reluctantly let her go for long enough to retrieve a wine bottle and glass from the kitchen.

"Do you prefer red or white?" I ask.

"White." Her answer is quick.

"Good, that's what I've got."

She eyes the single glass. "You're not having any?"

"Nah." I tuck the bottle under my arm, take her hand and lead her to the bathroom. "I don't drink while I'm in fight camp."

"Huh. So you don't drink, don't have sex, and you eat healthy. What do you do for fun?"

I shrug. "Hit people."

She gives me a dubious look. "Seriously. You must let loose somehow."

"I dunno." I set the wine down and start filling the tub. "To be honest, I don't usually have much free time."

Her brows draw together. "We've been spending time together. What would you normally be doing?"

"Watching videos of my opponent's previous fights."

"Oh." Her voice is small, and she hunches in. "Have I been getting in the way of your preparation?"

"Not at all." Laying my hands on her shoulders, I draw her close and feather a kiss over her lips, then another over her forehead. "I know Karson's style. I've fought him before, and I've also cornered Devon while the two of them fought. I don't need to watch a couple dozen videos. I know how he operates."

"So do I." She wraps her arms around my waist and rests her cheek over my heart. "He doesn't have a conscience, but he's also not invincible." Indecision crosses her features, as though she's debating whether to share a secret or not. But then her jaw firms and she seems to make up her mind. "He doesn't like to fight from the floor. He'll try to stay upright. If you get him down, you'll have the upper hand."

She's so serious. Her eyes are so sincere. I have to try really freaking hard not to smile. She's thinks this is something I don't already know. That she's passing on insider intel. But anyone who follows MMA could figure out the same thing if they spent a couple hours researching him. Still, the fact she's willing to betray his confidence for my sake sends warmth and affection fizzing through my chest, diffusing outward.

Caressing her cheekbone with the backs of my knuckles, I stare down at her in wonder. I could fall in love with this woman. She's everything I admire in a person. Passionate, loyal, determined. Not afraid to cut her own path.

"Jase," she whispers, as transfixed as I am.

I slide my palm around the curve of her cheek. "Yeah, baby?"

"The bath is about to overflow."

The bath is...?

Oh, fuck. Spinning around, I crank the tap off just as the water reaches the rim. Neither of us can get into it without water going everywhere, so I strip out of my jacket, roll up my sleeves, reach in and remove the plug, allowing it to drain.

"Why didn't you tell me earlier?" I demand, breathing heavily.

She makes an apologetic gesture. "I couldn't think properly with you looking at me like that."

The wind leaves my sails. I'd be a bastard if I grouched at her now. "Okay, I get that."

A shrill ring breaks the tension. I dry my hands and fish my phone from my pocket.

It's Erin. Just fucking great.

"Hop in," I suggest. "I'll be back in a moment." Taking the phone into the living room, and closing the door behind me, I answer. "What do you want?"

Tonight, I don't have the patience for her games. Not when there's a beautiful, naked woman waiting for me a couple rooms over.

"Jase." Her voice shakes, and she's talking quietly. "This whole thing has escalated too far."

"I couldn't agree more." She crossed a line when she sought out Karson. We both know she didn't do it because she was blown away by his charm. Going after my opponent was just another way for her to get back at me. Her mistake is in assuming I'll care.

"This war between us is silly," she continues, her pitch dropping lower. "Surely we can work it out. We were always good together, baby."

What. The. Fuck.

"No, Erin, we weren't. You and me aren't happening. Not ever. You stooped too low by letting your new man attack my girl. Don't call me again." I end the call then toss my phone on a chair and leave it there. Erin has never been good at understanding the word "no" and I don't want her interrupting my precious time with Lena again. Speaking of Lena, she's going to get a shoulder rub, and a foot rub, and the best damn cuddles she's ever had. I can't stop smiling at the thought of her.

Chapter 25

Scene 25

J ase

The next morning, when I try to sneak out of bed, Lena's arms tighten around me. "Don't go."

I kiss each of her closed eyelids. "Baby, I have to."

Her hand fists around my erection. "I can convince you to stay."

I'd much rather take her up on the offer than go for an eight mile run followed by an hour of pad and bag work. Gritting my teeth, I beg for strength. "It's fight week, cutie pie. I only have three more days of hard training before the big event. I need to give it my all." Nuzzling her neck, I trail kisses along her jaw until I reach her mouth. "Next week, I'm all yours."

Her eyes flutter open, nearly blinding me with their beauty, but mercifully, she releases her hold on my errant cock. "You are?"

"Yeah." My lips curve up. I love how excited she is by that prospect. My previous girlfriends have always been more anxious to be seen out and about with me than to actually spend time, just the two of us. "I always take a week off following a fight like this one. I won't be totally free, I'll have to meet with Seth and Nick to debrief, and the guys will want to do something together, but for the most part, I'll be yours."

She frames my face with her hands, looking up at me. "Maybe I'll take a couple days off, too. I think I deserve it."

"You should definitely do that, and I'm not going to let you out of this bed."

"Promise?"

I kiss her. "Fuck, yeah."

"Okay." She drops her hands and makes a shooing gesture. "Get going then. Go do shuttle runs or burpees or whatever torture Seth has in store for you."

I scramble from the bed before she changes her mind, tug on a tank top and shorts, and will my stiffy to do me a solid and go down before anyone sees. Fortunately, listening to sports podcasts while I pound out my run on the treadmill works wonders, and by the time I'm wrapping my hands at the gym, sex is far from my mind. Seth orders me to jump rope for twenty minutes, and I'm halfway through when the door bursts open and two uniformed police officers shove their way inside.

I'm so shocked, I forget to jump, and the rope whacks me across the shins, but I hardly notice. The officers stride across the floor toward me, their boots leaving tread impressions in the soft mats. One of them unclips a set of handcuffs from his belt. In my peripheral vision, I'm vaguely aware of Seth demanding to know what's going on, but I don't need to ask. The truth dawns on me with terrible clarity.

Erin went to the cops.

I didn't leap to do her bidding, and this is the punishment. She wants to see me locked away, my mugshot plastered across the papers and my name in the headlines, alongside hers.

"Jason Rawlins," one of the cops says in a booming, authoritative voice. "You are under arrest for misdemeanor battery against Erin Daley."

I don't try to run. There's nowhere to go. Numbly, I allow them to cuff me. I'm meeker than a newborn kitten.

"I didn't do it," I tell them, knowing it won't make an ounce of difference. They're not here to hear my story. They're here to take me in and let Erin play out her twisted little game in the court of public opinion. "I'm innocent."

"Yeah, yeah." The officer with the cuffs drags my arms behind my back with more force than necessary. "Save it for the judge, scumbag."

His partner clears his throat. "You have the right to remain silent. Anything you say can and will be used against you in a court of law."

I tune out the rest of his words, catching Devon's eye. Beside him, Gabe's swarthy complexion is paler than usual. Seeing their faces does nothing to reassure me, so I seek out Seth. My coach's glare could shoot flames, but he's calm and collected.

"I didn't do anything illegal," I say, desperation creeping over me.

Seth nods. "We'll fix this, Jase. Don't say anything until your lawyer arrives. No matter what they offer you, don't open your fucking mouth. Understand?"

I swallow. "Yeah, I understand."

"Good." With that, he turns away, already making a call. The officers shove me toward the exit, pausing long enough to let me don my shoes before dragging me outside. The second the door opens, cameras flash and I instinctively duck to get away from them. Shit. Someone called the paparazzi. This is going to be all over the news in minutes. How will Lena react? Lena. My stomach revolts, threatening to throw up the omelet I had for breakfast.

"Hold it in," an officer snaps when I retch. He yells at a nearby photographer, throws the back of his police cruiser open, and when I don't move fast enough, he stuffs me in.

On the way to the precinct, the officers lob questions back over their shoulders, but I keep my promise to Seth and don't say a word. Even when I want to. They're insulting me, trying to press my buttons. They must've been told I'm a hothead, but they didn't count on how close-lipped I can be when it serves my purposes. It's only when they transfer me to a holding cell and one of them gleefully holds up a copy of an overnight tabloid that they finally get through to me.

The headline reads: "Pro MMA Fighter Jase Rawlins's Underhanded Tactics." Beneath it, there's a photo of Lena and I from the fundraiser. I'm holding her close, my lips touching her ear. The picture leaves no doubt we're an item. As I scan the text, a writhing ball of fury grows in my stomach. It goes on to say how I screwed my way into getting a prestigious public relations firm to help sweep abuse allegations under the carpet, and how I'd doubled down on general assholery by seducing my opponent's ex-girlfriend to throw him off balance.

"It's not fucking true," I growl, stalking across the cell and kicking the bench seat. "Lena has nothing to do with this shit."

"Doesn't look that way to me," the officer counters with a taunting smile. He's loving this. One of the bad boys of MMA is under his control, and it's probably the best thing that's happened in his pathetic life. He turns the tabloid and cocks his head, checking out the photo. "She's a hot piece of ass. Bet it wasn't a hardship to tap that."

Without thinking, I lunge forward, gripping the bars and spewing a stream of profanities, ending with, "Don't you fucking look at her. Don't think about her. Stay the fuck away from her, or I'll rip you to shreds."

Smirking, the officer backs off. "Might want to get that temper under control, buddy. Judges don't look too kindly on violent assholes with anger management problems. Especially ones who threaten law enforcement professionals." He gestures to a camera in the corner. One I hadn't noticed was there.

"Fuck off." Sinking onto the bench, I bury my face in my hands. How the hell has it come to this? I thought everything had turned around. That the worst of it was over. But this shit is just getting started, and I've dragged Lena down with me.

I curse and stomp around, feeling utterly helpless. I've screwed everything up for her. Lena's professional reputation is more important to her than anything else, and now I've muddied it. Will that company she was so excited about even take a second glance at her after I've tainted her?

"I'm sorry," I mutter, knowing she can't hear me but hoping she knows, nonetheless. "So goddamned sorry, cutie pie."

What had she told me the other day? She didn't like the limelight. Well, she'd be getting plenty of it now.

I'm ruining her life.

Lena believed in me. For the first time, someone other than my brothers from the gym had complete faith in me, and I dumped this mess on her. I should've known I could never have someone as good and sassy and witty as her. I don't deserve her, and now the universe is balancing itself out.

The best thing I can do for Lena is to stayaway.

Chapter 26

Scene 26

Lena

I've been in the office for long enough to fix a cup of coffee and switch my computer on when Adrian sweeps in, dressed all in black with a grim expression. Uh-oh. This can't be good.

"LaFontaine," he barks, his chest puffed up with self-importance. Whatever he has to say, it must be serious, because he hardly ever calls me by my last name unless he's about to dump a shit sandwich in my lap. I resist the urge to salute and stand at attention, instead straightening my skirt and meeting his burning gaze. Jeez, something has put a bee in his bonnet.

"What is it, Adrian?"

"Jase Rawlins has been arrested."

My heart pounds in my ears, and I'm pretty sure I've misheard him. Pressing my palm to my chest to calm the wild hammering, I ask him to repeat himself.

"You heard me," he says, closing the door behind him. Dread creeps up my spine. This is bad. Really bad. He approaches me with the kind of slow, rolling walk that might be menacing if he were taller or broader. "I don't know how you possibly made things worse, but congratulations, you did." His eyes narrow. "Is this your way of getting back at me because you didn't want him as a client?"

"No." My back is ramrod straight. Even if I want to puke, I'm not going to cower and plead for forgiveness. I did my best to fix Jase's public image, even if I may have broken the no-fraternization rule while I was at it.

He gestures for me to sit but I don't. He wants the advantage of height so he can look down on me, and I'm not about to give it to him. In my heels, I'm a good two inches taller than Adrian.

His expression darkens. "Even if you can salvage this situation, I doubt you'll have a job at the end of this." Pausing for a moment, he lets his words sink in.

Is he threatening to fire me? Can he do that just because I didn't pull off a miracle?

Then he plays his ace. "Especially if you've been sleeping with him."

"Excuse me?" Did he just accuse me of...? My jaw drops. I mean, it's true, but where does he get off suggesting that? We haven't been obvious about it.

Smirking, he grabs his phone, switches on the screen and shows me the headline. The room spins dizzyingly around me, and I finally sit because the alternative is to risk collapsing. There's a photo of Jase and me on the front page of a tabloid magazine. The headline suggests that he slept with me to get himself out of a tight situation. I clutch my stomach, tasting bile in the back of my throat.

"I—"

"I don't care what you have to say for yourself." He tucks the phone away. "The evidence is clear." Leaning forward, he puts his palms on my desk, towering over me. My hands are trembling and I slide them beneath my thighs so he can't see. "I thought you were better than that, Lena."

He's loving this. Being able to lord it over me. I can't believe I gave him the ammunition to do it.

"It didn't interfere with my job," I say weakly.

"Are you really stupid enough to think that matters?" He raises a brow. "You've called the reputation of this firm into question."

Oh, God. This is actually happening. I'm going to lose my job. Panic lances through me. My career is all I have. If I lose that, what will I do? Go crawling back to my parents?

Never.

"The only way you're ever going to have a future at this firm is if you fix this within the next twenty-four hours." He tweaks his tie, and his tone is deceptively casual. "Even then, I'm uncertain whether we'll be able to overlook your indiscretion."

My shoulders slump. I've given Adrian exactly what he wants. A way to keep me under his thumb forever, or get rid of me. Did he ever actually have any intention of letting me choose my own clients? Or would he have kept stringing me along even if I'd pulled this off without a hitch and kept my hands off Jase's muscular body?

Leaning back in my chair, I look up at him. His plump cheeks are flushed with victory. "Did you ever plan to let me choose my own clients?"

He seems taken aback by the question. Then he shrugs. "Not really, truth be told. You're too valuable where you are."

His betrayal is like an icy needle to the heart. I pinch the bridge of my nose and drag in a slow, deep breath, trying to keep myself together. But you know what? Fuck that. Why shouldn't I tell this piece of human garbage exactly what I think of him? I'll be miserable if I stay here—which may not even be an option—and based on the tabloid he showed me, I'd say my reputation is shot to hell all over the city. Why not have a little fun burning my bridges?

I stand, and with a single motion, sweep nearly everything from my desk onto the floor, missing the laptop by a hair. A dozen tiny crashes sound in the space between us and the color blanches from Adrian's face. Stalking around the desk, I put my painful heels to good use and look down my nose at him.

"Don't bother firing me. I quit." A pressure lifts from my chest. "Fuck, that feels good." Smiling, I say it again. "I quit, Adrian. Effective immediately." Grabbing my bag from the floor, I sling it over my shoulder. "Good luck finding a replacement."

Then I march from the room, adding an extra sassy sway to my hips because I feel like a goddamn boss bitch. One who has no job, an apartment she can't afford, and is about to bail her man out of jail.

"Lena, wait!" Adrian calls after me.

I don't stop. Dimly, I'm aware of clapping as I pass through a series of cubicles, and Breanna catcalls and whistles. I don't meet her eyes because I'm not a hundred percent sure what I'm doing, and if I stop, Adrian might catch up to me. I'm not going to let him talk me into anything. I'm done making other people look good. It's time I do something for myself.

Look out, Las Vegas. Lena LaFontaine is a free agent, and I'm coming to take what's mine.

Chapter 27

Scene 27

L ena

With three phone calls, I find out where Jase is being held, and with another, I arrange a deal with a bail bondsman. Then I'm on my way. Clenching the steering wheel harder than needed, I try to check my panic. Only last night, Jase held me while I slept. Now he's in a cell. This is a nightmare. He's supposed to be training. Being arrested and detained is the last thing he needs, and he certainly doesn't deserve it.

I find a park, hurry into the precinct and make my way to the appropriate desk. "I'm here to post bail for Jase Rawlins," I tell the woman behind the counter.

She looks at me over the top of her glasses, and raises a brow like she doesn't approve of what she sees. I don't care. All I care about is getting him the hell out of here.

"And who might you be?" she asks.

"I'm his girlfriend."

Her brows knit together. "I thought his girlfriend was the one who filed the charges."

She's read the papers. Go figure. "That's his ex-girlfriend."

"Oh, honey." She shakes her head at me. "No amount of fame or money is worth being knocked around. Take the opportunity to get out."

I suck in a deep breath and release it slowly, reminding myself she doesn't have all the facts. "Can I pay the bail now?"

Pushing her glasses up her nose, she checks something on the screen. "That will be ten grand."

I nod. That's what I'd expected, and it's what I discussed with the bail bondsman. I'm not worried about paying, because I know Jase can pay me back tenfold. Even if he couldn't, I'd still bust him out. I pay the fee, sign some papers, and I'm led to a waiting area while a uniformed officer—who seems disappointed by my presence—leaves to collect Jase.

I can't sit still while I wait. I'm too fidgety and impatient. So I go over to the window and lean against it as I search my phone to see how many articles have reported the arrest, and also how many mention me personally. I scroll through pages of headlines and photos—my social life made visible to the entire world. God, it makes me sick to think what will happen to my career now. Everything I've worked so hard for, flushed down the toilet. Every hospital pass I took from a colleague means nothing. As far as the greater population is concerned, I'm just the girl stupid enough to jeopardize everything to screw Jase Rawlins.

The thing they don't realize?

He's worth it.

Several minutes pass before the officer brings Jase to me. Racing over, I throw my arms around him, not caring who sees. He squeezes me back and buries his face in the crook of my neck. He's dressed in his gym clothes and smells like old sweat, but I don't care. He draws back, his gaze skimming my face and then down my body as if checking I'm all in one piece. Finally, his eyes meet mine. They're shuttered and cold, and I can't help but flinch away from him.

"You bailed me out," he rumbles in a low, soft voice.

"Of course I did." I rest my hands on his slim hips, but he steps away and they drop to my sides. An icy sense of dread prickles in a corner of my mind. "What's wrong, Jase?"

His hands become fists, and he looks out the window, avoiding eye contact. "You shouldn't have. You should have just left me here."

My pulse kicks up a notch. What is he talking about? Why on earth would I do that?

"I couldn't stand the thought of you squished into a cell like an animal, and your championship fight is this week. You need to train." My lips purse. "I thought you'd be happy."

He glances over my shoulder, scowls at someone, then drags me outside. On the street, he raises a hand to ward off a photographer and takes me into an alley, at which point I dig in my heels. I've hit my limit on the amount of random bullshit I can handle today.

"What the hell is going on in your head?" I demand.

Running a hand through his hair, Jase clacks his teeth together so loudly I can hear them. "I'll pay you back whatever it cost to get me out, but after that, you need to leave me alone."

My heart stops. "I beg your pardon?"

"Baby." He takes a shaky breath. "Lena." He reaches for my hands, but I yank them away and back up into a wall.

"Don't touch me until you explain yourself."

Raw despair makes his features harsh. "Cutie pie, you're not seeing things clearly."

Well, that's condescending as fuck. "I'm seeing things perfectly clearly," I snap back.

"No," he grits out. "You're not." He starts to move closer, then stops himself. "This is so hard. But here it is: I'm bad for you. If I didn't know it already, the proof is all over the internet. I'm dragging you down with me, and I can't live with that."

I sigh, impatient. "You're not dragging me down. I chose you, asshole."

"And I'm choosing not to be the reason your life is ruined," he replies.

Seriously, it's like arguing with a brick wall.

"I see things more clearly than ever." Crossing to him, I lay my palms on his chest and stare up at him, willing him to stay with me. "I'm falling in love with you, Jase."

He goes white. Not the response I'd hoped for, although I didn't think before opening my mouth.

"Lena, I—" His Adam's apple bobs, and he visibly gets a hold of himself. "You're an amazing woman," he says, which sounds oddly like rejection, "and I can't bear to see you be reduced because you believe in me." Gently, he disengages my hands from his chest and puts space between us. "That's why I've got to back away from you."

He lingers, as though torn between whether to leave or stay. I want to make the decision for him, but I can also understand why he's struggling with this. For so long he's wanted someone to be on his side, even if he never said it, and now that he finally has me, it's all blown up in my face. He feels responsible.

Finally, he turns and walks away. Even though I understand, his desertion crumples my knees and I gasp for breath, willing myself not to cry.

He can walk away, but that doesn't mean I'm giving up on him. Jase can't get rid of me that easily.

Chapter 28

Scene 28

Lena

Hell hath no fury like a woman pushed beyond her limit. It's time to go full stalker mode. Everything that's happened today came about because of two people: Erin and Karson. But Karson can't fix it, and even though I'd willingly go three rounds with him in my current mood, doing so wouldn't help. No, I need to direct my righteous anger at Erin. The one who started it all.

First, I drive to the gym. Jase is already here, so I slip in unnoticed and gesture at Gabe, who's the only one to look up when I enter. He glances at Jase, then crosses to me in lazy strides that defy the intensity of his eyes. Gabe Mendoza is a strikingly handsome guy in that quiet, brooding way. He's bigger than Jase, and has a darker skin tone thanks to his Argentinian heritage. He also never seems to smile. Including now.

"Thanks for bailing him out," he says. "Seth was going to do it, but you beat him there. I guess he had a harder time coming up with the cash."

The bail wasn't a problem for me. My parents are filthy rich and while I don't ever touch their money because it comes with too many strings, my family name is a powerful tool when it comes to getting a loan. After all, lenders don't need to worry about a LaFontaine failing to pay them back.

"No problem." I step closer and lower my voice. "Can I talk to you privately for a moment?"

"Yeah." He rolls his massive shoulders. "Just let me towel off. I'll see you outside." He pauses, as though weighing his words, then adds, "Think it's for the best if Jase doesn't see you."

The statement hurts, but I know he's right so I backtrack and wait near the gym entrance. When Gabe emerges, he's wearing a hoodie, shorts, and nothing on his feet. The tops of his feet are tattooed and I can't help cringing at the thought of the pain he must have endured to get them.

"You've got a plan," he says, as though he already knows all about it.

Crossing my arms, I hold his gaze. "I guess they call you 'The Mind-Reader' for a reason."

He doesn't seem to get the joke. "I don't read minds. I'm just observant."

Gee, I never would have guessed that.

"What are you up to?" he asks.

I don't quaver in the face of his question, delivered with absolutely no emotion. Would it kill the guy to give me a hint of what's going on in his head?

"Erin," I say, getting straight to the point. "What's her story? Do you know what actually happened to her? Because someone hit her, and it wasn't Jase."

He mirrors my posture, folding his arms over his chest, and his biceps strain against the fabric. "Why do you want to know?"

I tap my foot, impatient. "Because I'm going to fix this, but I can't without all of the information."

Gabe nods, and I think I see a glimmer of appreciation in his eyes, but it disappears so quickly I could have imagined it. "Erin started dating someone else not long after they broke up. His name's Will Jones. Nasty S.O.B. Couldn't tell you for sure, but he's probably the one who hit her. All Jase did was give her a safe place to spend the night. She went psycho on him when he didn't want to get back in the saddle. That enough detail for you?"

My brain is firing at the speed of light. "This Will guy, is he another fighter?"

Gabe's lips twitch. "How'd you guess?"

"Erin has a type. MMA bad boy." I pat his arm. "Thanks, Gabe. Take care of him for me."

His eyes widen at the contact, and I wonder how long it's been since anyone touched him outside of training. Unlike other UFC stars, he's never in the tabloids with women, and Jase hasn't mentioned him having a girlfriend, either. I'll have to ask. After I convince the hardhead to give us a chance.

He nods, and shifts from foot to foot. "See you around."

"Bet your ass you will."

With a wave, I return to my car. I drive home and I search for Will Jones on my phone. For the next hour, I pore relentlessly over his social media, traveling back a few days until I find shots of him with Erin. In some, they look happy, but in others, there's fear and uncertainty in her expression. It's not immediately obvious, but for someone who knows where to look, the signs are there. She's scared of this guy, which means he's probably the guilty party. If she wasn't such a heinous bitch, I might feel sorry for her, but I can't quite find it in me when she's responsible for our current situation.

Digging a bit deeper, I come across a picture of the couple time-stamped with the date she alleges Jase hit her. I download a copy to my phone, then make a call to my contact Serene at the district attorney's office. A promise of tickets to an upcoming Las Vegas Thunder hockey game is all it takes to convince Serene to peek into Will Jones's police history. A few minutes later, she informs me that officers have been called to Jones's house several times following complaints from the neighbors about domestic disturbances. Each time the police arrived, and the women they encountered refused to speak with them.

Things are beginning to make sense. Erin must have been stupid enough to hook up with Will, and when he hit her, she went to the press. But why did she lay the blame at Jase's feet? Was it because she was truly misguided enough to think she could blackmail him into getting back together with her? Or perhaps she was simply too scared of Will to say a word against him. If it's the former, I can't blame her for wanting Jase back. He's caring and thoughtful and hot. He's also about to be a big name in MMA if he wins the championship fight. But what exactly is it that's driving Erin? Unrequited love? Money? A thirst for fame?

Several hours and a lot of favors later, I have the answer. Erin has credit card debt. A lot of it. Apparently her job at the salon doesn't pay enough to cover her lifestyle. Her rent is due, her cards are maxed out, and her utilities are soon to be shut off. She's in trouble.

And I have the leverage I've been looking for.

The bitch is going down.

Chapter 29

Scene 29

Lena

    This time, when I arrive at the salon, I don't wait for Erin to be finished with her client. I march straight over and plant myself in front of her. "We need to talk."

Erin doesn't pause. She continues snipping. The woman in the chair has wide doe-like eyes and looks familiar from somewhere. An actress or a musician, perhaps.

"I don't have anything to say to you," Erin snaps.

I raise the folder of papers I printed off at home. "You'd better make time, or I'll call every one of my tabloid contacts and share what I have in this file." Cocking my head, I aim for menacing, but I've never successfully menaced anyone in my life. "Trust me, you don't want this getting into the wrong hands. It could paint you in a very bad light."

She must know I'm serious because she stops and lays her scissors down, sending a patently false smile to her client. "I'll be back soon, Natalie. Can I get you a coffee?"

"Yes, please."

I follow Erin into the kitchen, where she busies herself at the counter. Sitting, I unpack the evidence I've come armed with, beginning with the photos of her and Will Jones, including the one from the day of the incident, and then moving on to his record of police call-outs, and lastly, I stack her financial details on top. She glances over her shoulder and comes to a dead halt.

"What the fuck are you doing?" she demands, shooting a look at the door. "Anyone could come in."

I shrug. "Then we'd better make this fast."

Leaving the coffee half-finished, she sits opposite me. The moment her gaze lands on the financial slips, she pales. "How did you get these?"

"I have ways." Not strictly legal, but effective, and if ever there's a time to blur the lines, it's now. I lean forward, staring her down. She looks straight back, but there's a hesitancy in her face that wasn't there before. "Do you know what I see when I look at this?" I ask.

She scans the tabletop and turns her palms toward the ceiling, like she couldn't care less. I know better. She's practically vibrating with tension. "Why don't you tell me?"

I sigh. I hadn't really thought she'd make it easy, but I'd hoped. "I see someone with lots of debt and mediocre taste in men who saw a way out of a tight spot and went for it."

Her jaw juts forward. "That's not how it is."

"No? Then how is it?"

She doesn't speak, but I wait her out. I have experience with waiting people out, and she won't win this game. Finally, in a small voice, she asks, "What do you want from me? Why can't you leave me alone?"

She sounds so young and pitiful that even though she's the same age as me and freaking vindictive, I cover her hand with my own. Yeah, she's a shitty judge of character—not to mention sneaky and petty—but I feel for her.

"I can't let you ruin Jase's life," I say softly. "He's a good guy. You know he is. And he doesn't deserve to serve time for something he didn't do."

Tears well in her eyes and she blinks them back. "He could have fixed all of this if he just took me back. That's how it was supposed to happen. But no"—a sneer mars her pretty face—"he had to hook up with you." Her tone is bitter. "If he'd just gone along with my plan, we'd be fine." She looks me up and down. "What's the big deal with you anyway? You're a seven, at best. I'm a ten."

Ugh. So much for feeling sorry for her. I pull away.

"Here's what's going to happen," I tell her, because I don't want her to think she can worm her way out of this and come out on top. "You're going to withdraw the charges and issue a public apology."

Erin scoffs. "No way in—"

"Or," I interrupt, biting down on my fury, "I share this with every-body in my personal address book." In case she's suffering any delu-sions, I add, "There's a lot of media firepower in that book."

She blinks, and wrinkles her nose like she's chewing on a soap bar.

"After that, I'll send it to the police. Do you really want them thinking you've wasted their time with bogus accusations?"

Now she just looks sick to her stomach. Time to offer the carrot.

"If you do what I've asked, I'll pay off your credit card debt and six months' worth of rent. Free and clear."

She laughs, covering her mouth with her hand. "You had me going for a moment there. Where would you find that much money?"

The jab doesn't sting the way she wants it to. I've had years to get used to the disbelief. "My last name is LaFontaine. As in, Malcolm and Henrietta LaFontaine."

If she was white before, she's ghostly now. "You—what?"

I allow her a moment to digest this. "I don't see my parents often, but I have access to the LaFontaine millions." For Jase, I'd do anything, including reaching out to my parents. "Do what I want, and the debt collectors will stop knocking on your door."

"But I'll be publicly humiliated," she protests.

"Honey." I say the word in my most sugary, condescending tone. "That will happen either way."

"Fuck," she swears, eyeballing me with a combination of defeat and respect. "I underestimated you."

"You did. So, what's it going to be?"

She takes a deep breath, steeling herself, and nods. "I'll do it."

"Good." Gathering the papers, I prepare to leave, but hesitate. "Word to the wise, Erin. Ditch Karson. He's a bad guy."

"Yeah." Her eyes meet mine. "I know." She shakes her head. "I sure can pick them."

"Maybe go for a baseball player," I suggest. "They're easier to handle."

"You know what?" She perks up. "I think I will." Reluctantly, she offers me a manicured hand. "Nice doing business with you."

I shake, giving it an extra squeeze so she knows not to mess with me again, and then I walk away from her without a backward glance.

You're welcome, Jase Rawlins.

Chapter 30

Scene 30

J ase

It's been three days since Lena bailed me out and I sent her away with nothing to remember me by except a bank transfer with a simple note: "thank you for everything". It's been three grueling days of training, and three lonely nights where I barely slept a wink despite having worked myself to exhaustion. Dwelling on Lena is painful, so I've focused all of my energy into avenging her the only way I can—by pulverizing Karson Hayes on international television. I'm going to make the fucker regret being born.

Although I haven't spoken to Lena, I've seen her twice. She dropped by to speak with Gabe, Devon, and Seth, but didn't try to approach me—perhaps I hurt her too much, a possibility I hate with a passion. None of them mentioned it to me, and I didn't ask. Frankly, hearing what's going on with her would mess with my head, and I can't afford that right now. Not when I'm determined to crush her ex.

It's Thursday afternoon, the day before the big fight, and everyone else has finished training. I should have, too. To be honest, I probably shouldn't be training at all today, but I need something to occupy my mind and everyone seems to sense it. Even hard-ass Seth hasn't tried to send me home. He just glowers disapprovingly and keeps reminding me not to overdo it.

I'm practicing my setups for a right overhand punch when Devon and Gabe come out of the changing room and cross over to me. Devon lays a hand on my shoulder while Gabe steps between me and the bag, narrowly avoiding a shot to the temple. He catches my fist and pushes it down to my side.

"This is an intervention," Devon says. "We're taking you back to your place, and we're going to watch some TV and chill."

I try to shake him off. "Not interested."

"We. Don't. Care," Gabe enunciates clearly.

"You've done enough, bro." Devon claps me on the back and steps out of reach, reading my mood. Gabe, on the other hand, stands steady. He doesn't care if he cops a punch. He's got something to prove to the world. Always has, always will. I guess being shouldered with a Golden Gloves champion for a father gives him a lot of expectation to live up to.

"We need to ice your hands and shins and go over your mental game," Devon continues. "Seth is coming too."

"He is?" This stuns me. Things must be serious for Seth to leave the gym. He practically lives here. None of us have even seen the guy's home, and sometimes I wonder if he just crashes on the gym floor. He's a great trainer, but he has even less of a personal life than we do. "Okay, I'll come."

I remove my gloves, grab my stuff, and follow them to the cars. We drive to my place, with Seth promising to be close behind. Inside, I leave Gabe and Devon in the living room while I shower. When I return, they're on the sofa, watching the sports news, and two buckets of icy water are waiting for me. Dunking a fist into each of them, I wince at the bitter chill.

"Why are we watching this?" I ask. Usually we watch re-runs of the opponent's last few fights and talk strategy at this point in the training camp, staying far away from the news in case they mention the upcoming event and psych us out.

Devon checks the time. "You'll see in a moment."

The door opens, and Seth strides in. "Your security is shit."

"Good to know," I mutter, having previously been under the impression it was top of the line.

"Shh," Devon hisses, and then the setting on the TV changes and Erin appears.

The air rushes from my lungs, and I snatch my fists from the frigid water, balling them. "What the fuck?"

I try to understand what's happening. Are they going to interview Erin about the assault charge? It would be perfect timing to throw me off for tomorrow. But if that's the case, why would my brothers make me watch it when I might otherwise have been able to remain oblivious until after the fight?

"Just wait," Gabe says.

The presenter finishes introducing her and gives the back story of her accusations, then finally invites her to speak.

I tear my gaze from the screen. "I don't want to hear this." I search desperately for the remote, but someone has hidden it. "Seriously, guys. Change the channel."

"Just watch," Seth grunts, and I do. Because when Seth speaks, we all listen.

What comes next shocks the hell out of me. Erin tells the truth. With tearful eyes, she admits to having lied about me hitting her. Then she apologizes. She fucking apologizes to me on live TV. What on earth is going on?

I watch, rapt, as she goes on to explain that the creep who assaulted her was actually Will Jones, but she'd hoped she'd be able to use the situation to manipulate me into taking her back.

I can't believe this is happening.

She's humiliating herself in front of the nation, and in doing so, saving my ass. But Erin doesn't do anything selflessly, so what is she up to?

"Why?" My voice is husky, but fortunately my brothers seem to understand.

"This is all Lena," Devon explains, and holds up a hand to silence anything I'm about to say. "I know you don't want to talk about her, but she made us promise you'd watch it so your mind would be clear for the fight tomorrow."

"She..." I'm struggling to wrap my head around this. "She did? But how'd she get Erin to back down?"

I'm the luckiest bastard in the world. I pushed an amazing woman away and she still saved my sorry self. Jesus, I hope I haven't ruined my chance with her permanently.

Is two weeks too soon to be in love?

Fuck no. I'm crazy about her, and she must feel the same way, right? Why else would she do all she has to fix my screwed-up life?

Devon shrugs. "No idea, and we asked. She didn't want to say."

A reluctant smile tugs Gabe's lips. "She's as stubborn as you."

My phone rings, and I rush to answer it, praying it's Lena. Caller ID shows it's only Nick, and disappointment floods me. I should've known it wouldn't be her.

"What's up?" I ask.

"Great news, buddy. I just got off the phone with your lawyer, and the charges against you have been dropped."

Gratitude overwhelms me. Lena. She's responsible for this. If I live to be a hundred, I'll never be able to thank her enough. "That's amazing, thanks."

"No problem." He pauses, then adds, "Rest up tonight. I'll see you tomorrow."

Ending the call, I scan the faces around me. "The charges have been dropped."

"Yes!" Devon fist-pumps.

Gabe's rare smile widens.

Seth just watches me with steady green eyes. "She's a fine woman. You'd better hold onto her."

I nod to my mentor. "I plan to."

Chapter 31

Scene 31

L ena
You know how some mornings you wake up and have this feeling that everything is going to change? That was me this morning. It's the day of Jase's championship fight and also the day of my interview with Englewood. To say I was shocked when they called and requested to meet with me would be an understatement. I was astounded. I honestly believed I'd burned all my bridges when I quit my job after those damning articles were published. I even asked the intern who contacted me to double check she had the right person.

And that's why it's totally surreal to be sitting opposite Maria Englewood, wearing a stylish yet respectable pantsuit and discussing the possibility of my future employment at her firm. Maria Englewood is one of the most distinguished women I've ever met. She's slightly shorter than average, with dark hair in a sleek topknot. Her dress is designer but not flashy, and she has this way of weighing every word she says that gives the impression she's always the smartest person in a room.

To be fair, she's definitely the smartest person in this room. I can only aspire to her heights. She represents female CEOs, politicians, and other power houses, and also has a pro bono legal clinic that specializes in domestic and family law. In short, she rocks, and I want to work for her. Hell, I want to be her.

"Lena," she says, after we've been through the standard interview questions and I've somehow answered them without turning into a total fangirl, although I've had to rest my hands in my lap so she can't see them shaking. "I admit, I wasn't sure how this conversation would go. Your experience isn't directly in line with what we do here, but I love your passion. You have the kind of fire and enthusiasm we need at Englewood."

Oh. My. God. Did Maria Englewood just compliment me?

My head swims and I'm dangerously close to crying happy tears.

"Thank you," I reply.

She folds her hands in front of her and cocks her head, studying me with intelligent eyes. "There's just one more thing I need to ask about."

My stomach sinks. She wants to know about the debacle with Jase. Of course she does. It makes me look like a liability.

"I respect you, Lena, so I'm going to come straight out and ask. What happened with Jase Rawlins?"

There it is. The kiss of death. I'm done before I even have a chance.

"That situation was messy," I say. "I didn't want to take on Jase as a client, but I was pressured into it. Everything was going well until Monday, and you'll have seen that the woman responsible publicly apologized yesterday and withdrew charges." I sigh, and decide I may as well throw myself fully off the cliff. "The truth is, I fell in love with him." Her expression is impossible to read, so I power on. "I don't want you to think I make a habit of hooking up with clients. This was a one-time thing. Jase is special."

Maria nods, still not giving anything away. Then she finishes her glass of water and shuffles her papers into a stack. Is she dismissing me?

When she stands, I do too. "Thank you for the opportunity." I head for the door. As I open it, her voice stops me.

"Lena, I'll see you at eight a.m. on Monday."

Wait, what?

I glance over my shoulder, and she smiles at me. "Welcome aboard."

"Oh my gosh," I stammer. "Thank you. I'll be here."

I walk out with my spirits so high I could touch the ceiling. I have a new job. I'm finally going to be working with the type of clients I want. My idol just gave me a second chance. Slumping against the elevator wall, I stare at the ceiling. Maria Englewood won't regret hiring me. I'll make sure of it. I'm going to be the best new recruit ever.

By the time I reach my apartment, I'm still soaring, but I come to a halt when I spot two men loitering by my door. My heart leaps to my throat. I take one step, then another, relaxing when I recognize Devon. He's with Gabe, and they both look up as I approach.

"What are you doing here?" I ask, trying to sound casual but missing the mark. "Does this have something to do with Jase? Is he okay?"

"We're here to take you to the fight," Devon says without his usual grin. In fact, everything about their body language says they're both on edge. "Put on your prettiest dress. We've got half an hour before we need to go."

"I'm not sure I understand." I slot the key into the lock and turn it. They both hustle inside. "Jase clearly said he didn't want to see me, so I wish him luck, but I'm not coming with you. I don't want to distract him."

I'd already planned to sit alone in bed and stuff my mouth with ice cream while streaming the fight online. The thought of watching him in the ring makes me sick to my stomach, but equally, there's no way I'd be doing anything else. I need to know what happens, and whether he's safe at the end.

"Oh, you're coming," Gabe tells me, grabbing me by the shoulders and looking me in the eye. "We've arranged everything. All you need to do is get ready, and we'll take care of the rest."

"But I—"

"No buts," Devon interrupts, glancing at the clock on the wall. "We need to be with our brother soon to help him prepare, which means you need to get a move on." He made a shooing motion. "Go."

Sensing that they'll drag me to the fight in my interview outfit if I don't do as they ask, I hurry to the bedroom and throw open my closet, searching the racks for something sexy but casual, and which another man didn't buy for me. I won't make that mistake again. Settling on a classic little black dress, I strap on some heeled sandals and darken my eyeliner, then wipe off my neutral lipstick and replace it with my favorite red. Ready, I let them sweep me out of the apartment.

A sleek sedan is waiting at the curb, and they guide me to it. We're mostly quiet during the drive, although I do my best to uncover their plan. The way they shrug and grunt makes me wonder if they even have one. Once we arrive at the venue, a guard lets us in the rear entrance, where the fighters are getting ready. Devon leads the way to a closed door with "Rawlins" scrawled in marker across it. Gabe stays by my side, but nods to the woman waiting in the hall. She's gorgeous, with brown skin, crinkled hair, and curves for days. She's also wearing a Jase Rawlins supporter hoodie, with his face and "The Wrangler" stamped on the front. When we reach her, Gabe stuns me by dropping a kiss on her cheek.

He turns to me. "Lena, this is my best friend, Sydney. You're going to hang with her tonight." Without further ado, he and Devon enter the room and leave Sydney and I in the corridor.

She offers me a smile. "Call me Syd. You must be Lena." She scans me up and down, but not in an unfriendly way. "Gabe's told me a lot about you."

He has? He hardly seems the chatty type.

"Best friend, huh?" I ask, because based on the way her cheeks flushed when he kissed her, she's into him as more than a friend.

But she just nods. "Yeah, Gabe and I go way back. Come on, I'll show you to our seats." As we walk, she talks. "Gabe and I grew up in the same neighborhood and went to the same schools." She sighs. "We used to be inseparable."

I have to increase my pace to keep up. Though she's shorter than me, Sydney can move fast. "Used to be?"

She slants me a wry look. "The only thing he's inseparable from these days is his boxing gloves. I don't know if you've noticed, but MMA is more than a sport or a job to these guys. It's an obsession."

"Yeah, I'm getting that impression."

She pushes an unmarked door and suddenly we're in the arena. It's massive, with a high ceiling, grandstands, and a cage in the center. The seats are starting to fill, and the atmosphere is buzzing with excitement. It hits me now how real this is. Before long, Jase is going to walk the aisle between the seats and enter the ring. He'll face off against Karson, and you can bet your ass they're both going to bring the pain.

I'm not sure if I can handle this.

"Oh, shit. I can't." I stop walking, and Sydney spins to face me.

"It's okay," she says, reaching over to thread her fingers through mine. "I know what you're going through. I've been there. But you need to remember that our boys are tough. Jase has trained harder for this fight than any other, and if you've ever seen him, you know he usually kicks ass. Gabe says it's like he's possessed."

She squeezes my hand, and I pray my palm isn't too sweaty because she's being really nice and I don't want to pay her back by perspiring all over her.

"Jase will give everything he has out there, and you have to have faith it'll be enough." Her lips kick up. "Think you can do that? If not, tell me now because I also snuck in a flask of tequila and a pair of tinted glasses." She leans closer and murmurs, "They're great for pretending to watch when you're really shitting yourself."

Her honesty startles a laugh from me. "I think I'll be okay," I tell her. "But you're kind of great, did you know that?"

She flashes her perfect teeth. "I try."

My legs release from their knee-lock and I follow her to a pair of reserved seats immediately in front of the cage. Possibly the best seats in the entire place.

I whistle. "Impressive."

"I know, right?. The boys always make sure I get to watch in style."

We sit, and Sydney draws a copy of the fight card from her purse, passing it to me. I scan the names, quickly finding the only one I care about.

"Jase is last." That means I have to sit through every undercard fight before we get to him. The nerves are going to kill me.

"That's because he's the main event. It's a big honor for him."

"I know, but that doesn't make me any less queasy."

She slings an arm around me. She's a very touchy person, which reminds me of Breanna, and I instinctively like her more for it. A subtle scent washes over me. What is that? I sniff.

"It's disinfectant," she explains, and I immediately feel like a weirdo for being so obvious about it. "I'm a surgical resident at Sunrise Hospital."

"That's awesome." She must be crazy smart.

Sydney shakes her head. "No, awesome is what you did for Jase."

"Thanks." I'm a little uncomfortable with her compliment, but it's sweet. "You know what?" I ask. "I've got a good feeling about you. I think we're going to be friends."

She grins back. "I agree."

We settle in and it doesn't take long before thefirst fight is announced. The ball of tension in my gut winds tighter, and Iprepare myself for a long evening.

Chapter 32

Scene 32

Jase

I'm always jittery before a fight, but tonight I'm driving myself crazy. I pace restlessly, shadowbox, and get told several times not to warm up too early. I know I shouldn't, but nerves are eating at my insides. This fight is a big deal. Even before I met Lena, it was going to be the biggest of my career so far, but now my girl's honor is on the line. I will win this fight for her. I intend to smear Karson Hayes's blood all over the floor and roll around in it. Then, and only then, will I deserve to have her back.

As time passes, the back corridor rooms empty. First the amateurs leave, then the pros. Eventually, a medic comes by to check my blood pressure and make sure I'm uninjured. An hour before I'm due to make my grand entrance, Seth wraps my hands. Though I'm capable of doing my own, wrapping his fighter's hands is a ritual for Seth at events like this. It calms him. He can be a raging psycho otherwise.

"You got this," he murmurs as he winds tape around my knuckles, then loops it between each of my fingers. "You trained hard, just stick to the game plan. Get him on the ground and keep him there. Don't let up. Karson is best on his feet. He's a distance striker. If you give him the chance, he'll toy with you. Don't let that happen. You hear me?"

I nod. "Loud and clear."

He puts the finishing touches on one hand and moves to the other. "He'll try to piss you off, and get in your head. Ignore him. If he says anything, all you hear is 'blah blah blah.' Got it?"

"Yeah." I already know this. Karson will want to run his mouth. Talk smack about Lena. He'll want to put me at a disadvantage. For some people, anger motivates them to victory, but it clouds my vision. I need to keep a clear head.

"You remember how to start?"

"Throw a strike to catch him off guard, then take him down."

"Atta boy." He finishes my wraps and jerks his chin at someone over my shoulder. "Dev, come and spar with Jase. Nice and easy. I want him limbered up and ready to go, but not tired."

"Yes, sir." Devon salutes him, but Seth doesn't smile. In fact, he looks ready to crack a jaw. "Tough audience."

Devon slips on a pair of padded boxing gloves to lessen the impact of his strikes and moves in. I bounce on the balls of my feet and, when he's ready to go, throw an overhand punch. Devon ducks, and I trip him. He falls neatly to the floor and rolls, coming back up before I can pounce. Excitement blazes in his eyes. Devon is crazy when he fights. He seems to love being in the cage regardless of whether he's doing the pounding or being pounded. That's how he got his nickname: Dangerous. There's nothing more dangerous than a fighter who doesn't care if he gets hurt.

I strike again, and he counters. We circle each other, and Seth barks out orders to me while Gabe coaches Devon. By the time we stop, a sheen of sweat covers my body and my muscles are loose. All except the ones in my stomach. My fucking anxiety hasn't gone anywhere. Aren't I supposed to be above that shit by now?

The promoter's assistant sticks his head through the door and tells us we're due out in five minutes. Seth helps me into my fight jacket and rubs Vaseline over my cheeks and forehead. My heart is a steady thump in my chest. Despite being nervous, I've done this routine plenty of times before, and I know what comes next. It's all so familiar to me. Gabe and Devon check the contents of my spit bucket. Ice, liquid adrenaline, water, Vaseline, mouthguard, first aid kit. They form a line behind me, with Seth at the head and Devon at the rear. I jog lightly on the spot to stay warm.

The assistant returns, and checks my hands to make sure we're obeying regulations, then gives the nod of approval. Together, we make our way through the corridors, past a number of trainers from other gyms who nod and mutter encouragements. We pause out of sight of the arena and wait. After a moment, my walk-out song plays over the loudspeakers.

Immediately, adrenaline floods my body, the same way it always does when I hear this song. It's my cue to enter warrior mode. I rock in time to the beat and wait for the perfect moment, right as the music crashes down from a crescendo. I stride out, chin up, shoulders back, and inject every bit of swagger I can into my walk. The audience roars for me. I don't smile, because this moment sets the tone of the match. Up ahead, Karson is already in the cage, waiting. He waves his fists in the air and stomps his foot. He's always been a show pony.

Asshole.

Then I hear a familiar voice amid the crowd.

"Jase!" she screams. "Smash him, Jase! You've got this in the bag!"

Glancing down, I spot Lena. Our eyes lock, and a powerful charge passes between us. I nod to her, and a strange calm descends over me. She's right. This fight is mine. Because I'm fighting for her, and you know what that means?

I can't lose.

I'm fucking invincible.

She'll be waiting for me after, and I don't care how sore I am, I'm going to keep her in bed all weekend. I'll fuck her so thoroughly, she can't remember there's a world outside the bedroom.

Seconds later, I'm in the cage. The announcer yells my name, and then Karson's. The umpire summons us to the center and gives the usual spiel. We don't bump fists. Karson doesn't deserve that honor. We each return to our corner, then a beeper sounds, and I rush forward.

Chapter 33

Scene 33

L ena
   As the fight begins, I'm equal parts mesmerized and horrified. Jase is like poetry when he moves. Beautiful, lethal poetry. There's no tentativeness as his fist plows straight into Karson's face and I shriek my support. Karson slams a knee into Jase's gut and I interlock my fingers with Sydney's. Jase doesn't react to the strike, but he does something with his feet, and the next thing I know, Karson is falling to the ground, taking Jase with him. They roll and struggle for the dominant position and I clutch Sydney even harder.

Jase comes out on top, and I whoop. Rearing back, he bludgeons Karson with one of those massive hands that have held me so gently. He hits him again, and again. Karson tucks his chin and tries to shield his face. Then, somehow, he shifts and flips Jase to the bottom.

I scream. "Get up! Get the fuck up!" And when Karson punches Jase's gorgeous face, I squeeze my eyes shut. "Oh God, oh God, oh God."

The crowd cheers, and I'm afraid to look. Then a ding sounds and Sydney's voice is in my ear.

"It's okay, Lena. The round has ended. Jase is fine."

Opening my eyes, I blink until my vision readjusts. In the cage, Seth is up in Jase's grill, talking and gesturing with firm movements. Devon is icing his legs, and Gabe is smearing something over a cut at his temple.

"What's he saying?" I ask Sydney, although I have no idea why I think she knows the answer.

But she eyes them thoughtfully. "My guess is Seth is telling Jase to get him in a chokehold and force him to tap out."

"How do you work that out?"

She looks over at me. "A couple of things. After a while, you get good at reading Seth's hand gestures. Also, choking people is Jase's specialty, so it's a pretty safe bet."

I shudder. Legal or not, there's something scary about having a lover who's known for choking his opponents. The umpire orders the others out of the cage and the second round begins. Whatever Seth said, it's fired Jase up because he launches himself at Karson and knocks him to the ground. Grabbing him from behind, he wraps his legs around Karson's waist and loops his elbow under his chin. Karson throws his weight around, trying to dislodge Jase, but he's like a pit bull and doesn't let go. There's a steeliness in his eyes I recognize, and also a gleam of triumph.

He's got this.

Karson can't shake him. The other fighter bucks and flails to no avail. Finally, his face red, he taps the floor. The umpire ends the fight and hurries to separate them. Karson bends over, gasping for air, and Jase leaps nimbly to his feet, waving a fist. I scream, and so does everyone else.

Then he turns and looks right at me. Heat shoots straight to my core. He's sweaty and bleeding, every muscle popping like crazy, and I want him to pin me against a wall and fuck me harder than ever before. But then his crew swarm, and his gaze is torn from mine.

"Damn, girl," Sydney exclaims, bumping my shoulder. "That was hot."

It was. So hot I feel like I'm going to crawl out of my skin with want. My body aches for him, and so does my heart. I want to go to him, right now, but the umpire is taking his hand and raising it above his head. A pretty girl in a tube top and miniskirt fastens the world's largest belt around his waist and then someone is shoving a microphone in front of him. The volume of the audience falls, as they all wait for him to speak. He's grinning. The biggest, most stupidly sexy grin I've ever seen.

"Hi, everyone," he says, his tone uneven, as though he hasn't caught his breath yet. "This is such an honor. I wanna thank my coach, Seth Isles, and my training partners from Crown MMA. I couldn't have done it without you." At this, both Gabe and Devon hit their fists to their hearts. He looks over at Karson, who's sulking in the corner. "I also wanna thank Karson for bringing his A-game."

Karson glares like he wants to flip him off, but nods graciously.

"But there's also someone else I need to thank," Jase says, and then his eyes are on me.

I go still inside. He holds my gaze, and I wish I was closer so I could see what's going on behind those slate gray eyes.

"A special woman gave me the motivation I needed to pull through."

Oh. My. God. He's talking about me.

Sydney gives my shoulder a push, and hisses, "Go to him."

But I don't move. I can't. My feet are rooted to the ground.

In the cage, Jase clears his throat, and when he speaks again, his voice is thick with emotion. "I always thought love was a distraction, but it turns out it's the most powerful motivator of all." Then he hands the microphone to someone else and stalks toward me.

My legs are jelly. My spine, too. This man has turned all of me to goo. I can't even tell how the people in the arena are responding to this unexpected turn of events because I can't hear them anymore. All I can hear is the drumming of my pulse in my ears.

Jase stops in front of me and reaches out ahand. I take it, and he yanks me upright. I can see his eyes now, and they'reso freaking deep and warm, and the emotion in them rocks me, but he holds myarms so I don't fall. Movements around us blur into the background. I stare athim, and he stares right back. The moment seems to go on forever, and I wonderwhich of us will be the first to break it.

Chapter 34

Scene 34

J ase

I am the fucking super lightweight champion. But better than that, I feel like a man who's worthy of Lena. Maybe it's the adrenaline talking. Shit, maybe it's just the caveman part of me that wanted to vanquish her ex, but I'm on top of the world, and all I care about is that Lena keeps looking at me this way every day for the rest of our lives.

Fuck, she's perfect, and her eyes say everything her words haven't. She wants me. She's proud of me. She loves me.

"Lena," I rasp, smoothing a battered hand around the sweet curve of her face. "I know what you did for me."

Her lips part, but no sound emerges. I want to kiss them. I want to claim those pouty red lips in front of everyone here, but I need to talk to her first.

"This was all for you," I tell her, willing her to understand. "I won for you."

Her eyes widen, and her tongue darts out to wet her lips. My cup is suddenly too tight at my groin. I bend so my mouth hovers above hers.

"I love you," I whisper. "And I want to be with you. I'm sorry for pushing you away. I promise, if you give me another chance, I'll never let you out of my sight again."

"Jase, I—"

"Wait a sec." I hold a finger to her lips. I need to finish this properly. But she licks my finger and heat lashes through me. My cup situation changes from uncomfortable to downright painful, and I drop my hand away. "You also gotta know that if you say yes to me, that's it. I'll destroy any other man who dares touch you." I hear the steel in my voice, and know she does too. Does it make me a Neanderthal? Fuck, yeah. Do I care? Not a bit. This is my woman, and I'll challenge anyone who says otherwise. Except for her, of course.

Her lips lift, her palms cup my face, and then she kisses me. Hell, yes. Hell, yes. Finally, I can own her lips like I've been dying to ever since I first touched her. Love and adrenaline fuel me, and I hoist her up. She wraps her legs around me but our mouths don't separate. Our tongues tangle, and I'm drunk on the taste of her. The smell of her. The urge to fuck and mark and claim.

Supporting her weight with one arm, I wave to the crowd with the other and carry her back down the aisle, out to my changing room, where I lock the door and back her against it. Bracing an arm above her head, I lean down and slide my tongue over her swollen lips. Her eyes are glazed, and she's panting. Her fingers trail down my abs, and I shudder at her touch.

"I love you," I tell her again. "I'd conquer the world for you. Whatever you had to do to make Erin back down, I'll make it up to you, I swear."

"I love you too." She half moans, half whispers, and my eyes automatically search hers for the truth. Finding it, I press myself against her and rock. Then, cursing, I rip off the damned cup and toss it aside.

She giggles. "Problem?"

"None at all." I rest my cheek on the top of her head, holding her close. "I'm gonna spend every day trying to be worthy of you."

Her palms slide up to rest over my heart. "You already are. As for Erin, we can talk about it later. There are other things I'd rather be doing now."

I'm not worthy of her—no one is—but it's sweet that she believes it, and I'm totally down for her suggestion. My cock stiffens, straining to get to her, and she must feel it because she eases a hand between us and wraps her fingers around it, ripping a groan from me.

"I want you in me," she murmurs, pumping her hand.

My hips buck. I'm already so close. God, if she keeps that up I'm going to snap like an animal. "No, baby. We need to take it slow this time."

However hard this is—pun fully intended—I'm determined to do it right. But then she takes my hand with her free one and shoves it under the hem of her dress.

"Fuck." She's not wearing panties, and she's soaked.

"Forget about slow," she says, riding my hand as I slip fingers through her slickness. "Take me how you want."

I nuzzle her neck, dropping kisses along her collarbone. "You sure?"

She lifts my face so we're looking each other in the eye. "One hundred percent."

Thank God.

I ruck up that teasing little skirt, shove my shorts down and sink into her. Balls deep. She gasps and tightens around me. She's just as turned on as I am. Maybe more. I could get used to this. Thrusting in and out, I strum her clit with my thumb, loving the way she whimpers and cries out. She feels so good. So. Damn. Hot.

Desperation creeps over me. I slam into her, and her back arches, her fingernails digging into my shoulders. I push harder, faster, driving her wild, and then she's breaking apart in my arms and I'm holding her together and spilling every-fucking-thing I have into her. My thighs shake, my cock jerks, and I growl her name. Our foreheads press together and we stare into each other's eyes.

I love her.

I love this woman. My Lena.

She chuckles breathlessly. "When can we do that again?"

I capture her lips. "Any time you want, baby."

Chapter 35

Scene 35

G^{abe}

G abe
        As Jase makes up with his girl and carts her from the arena amid a roar of approval, a pang of longing shoots through me. Despite my best intentions, I find myself seeking out Sydney.

God, she looks good tonight. She always does. Her cheeks are rosy, eyes bright, and she's watching the couple leave with a good deal of satisfaction, but possibly a little envy, too. I can relate. I wish I could lay claim to Sydney and her luscious curves and brilliant mind the way Jase just laid claim to Lena, but I can't. She's made it clear that when she decides to get serious with a man, she needs to be his priority. Unfortunately, I have too much to live up to, too much still to achieve, to give her the attention she deserves.

Someday soon, she'll find a guy who can give her what she needs, and the thought shreds me inside even though I know I'm not right for her. After all, on what planet would it make sense for a doctor, someone who dedicates her life to helping people, to hook up with a brute like me? They might call me "The Mind-Reader" because of my smarts and speed in the cage, but when it comes to anything else, I'm no match for Sydney, and we both know it.

That doesn't make it any easier to know that one day I'll have to step aside and let some other guy be the one to make her smile. The one to touch her. Even thinking about it makes me so furious, I want to throw her over my shoulder and follow Jase the hell out of here. But when she does find that guy, I'll back off. For her sake.

Even if I know there'll never be another girl for me.

Chapter 36

Scene 36

A Year Later

Jase

The tattoo machine hovers above the center of my chest.

"You're sure, man?" the artist asks, giving me one last chance to change my mind.

"Hell, yeah." No way I'm backing out of this. I'm going to give Lena a proposal she'll remember for the rest of her life.

The tattooist, a guy by the name of Mercy, shakes his head. "She must be some woman."

I grin as he sets the machine to my skin and it starts buzzing. "She's amazing." Tiny needles plunge into me, forming a black line. "She's so out of my fucking league."

Mercy raises a brow but doesn't look away from his work, and his hands remain perfectly steady. "You're Jase Rawlins. No one is out of your league."

I laugh, because he doesn't get it. Lena isn't the one who's lucky in this relationship, I am—although I do make sure she gets as many top-notch orgasms as she can handle. It's no less than she deserves for loving my stupid ass and for striking the devil's bargain with Erin to save me. Not that I let her go to her parents with her hand out for my sake. Fuck, no. As soon as I found out what she'd agreed to, I paid off Erin's loans myself. It was a small sum for me, and well worth it to preserve Lena's dignity.

"Tell me about her," he says, finishing the outline of an "L" and moving on to the next letter. I hope Lena understands what it means for me to have her name over my heart. I wish it could be larger, but unfortunately most of the real estate in that area is already taken.

"She's perfect," I say, grinning like a goober. "Clever, loyal, beautiful, feisty as hell."

"Sounds like my kind of girl."

"Hands off," I reply, good-naturedly. "She's all mine."

He laughs. "I'm not gonna fight you for her, bro. I'm smarter than that." He continues working and I stay on my back and answer questions about my most recent fight. It's just as well I don't have any in the near future or Seth would flip out at the sight of my new tattoos. As it is, I'm expecting plenty of jibes from my brothers. When the artist finishes, he repeats care instructions I've heard a dozen times before. I barely listen, too distracted by the nerves buzzing in my stomach. Persistent and loud.

I'm going to ask Lena to marry me. What if she says no?

She won't. She loves me. Nevertheless, the nerves settle in. They won't go anywhere until after I hear a 'yes' from the lips of the woman I love.

Leaving the parlor, I head straight to the jewelers. I've already chosen a ring, and they've been resizing it for me. Fortunately, Sydney knew Lena's ring size. Apparently that's something women talk about. She's been an absolute godsend the past few weeks, and to top it off, she's keeping Lena busy at a spa until I'm ready to woo her tonight.

She's going to be so fucking wooed she never looks at another man again.

I pay the jeweler an exorbitant amount and receive a small black box in return. Opening it, I gaze down at the sparkling white-gold diamond ring nestled inside. It's flashy, but elegant. Sexy, but not over the top. I think it suits her, but then, what do I know?

When I arrive back at my place, my friends are already there. Gabe, Devon, Seth and Nick are on board with my big plan and they've started decorating. There's a trail of red petals from the entrance to the twin glass doors that open onto the deck, and Devon glances up from where he's scattering them.

"Can I see your ink?"

Shaking my head, I admire his handiwork. "Sorry, brother, no can do. Lena is going to be the first to see it."

He finishes with the petals and straightens. "You're so under her thumb that I'm embarrassed for you."

"That's only because you don't get the benefits."

He winks. "For your sake, I hope there are a lot of benefits."

"Oh, there are." Lena and I are combustible together. But even better is the way she makes me feel like I'll never be alone again.

Never be unwanted or misunderstood. Fuck, I love her. "Where're the others?"

Devon jerks his head toward the deck. It's currently empty because I don't have much free time to laze in the sun, but Lena has been dropping hints about getting a table and sunchair for weeks now. I hope she likes my surprise.

"Seth and Gabe are assembling the table, and Nick is..." He shrugs. "Supervising, I guess."

I wince. Nick is a great manager, but he isn't one to get his hands dirty—a fact that probably isn't going over well with the others. "I'd better make sure everything is coming along all right."

Outside, Seth is putting the finishing touches on a kitset table while Gabe is piecing together the chairs. Nick is hovering over him, offering suggestions, and Gabe's jaw cranks tighter with each one.

"How's it coming?" I ask, just as Nick—thankfully—takes a phone call.

"Nearly there," Seth replies. "If you give me a hand, we can move this wherever you want it."

Grabbing the opposite end, I heft it up and together we shift it to the center of the deck, into a position where I can see Devon approaching with his trail of petals. I turn to join Gabe, but Seth stops me with a hand on my shoulder.

"You ready?" he asks, voice low. "Do you need to rehearse or something?"

"Nah. I've got this. But thanks."

He nods, expression serious. "The candlesticks are in a box in the kitchen, and Devon picked out your nicest dining ware, ready to go."

"Thanks. I owe you."

Seth seems to be taking this whole proposal business just as seriously as I am, and I can't help but wonder if it's because of how wrong things went for him in his marriage. Not that he's been terribly open about what happened.

"The tablecloth is laid out, too," he adds.

"I'll start setting the table if you want to finish up the chairs with Gabe," I say.

We part ways, and I head for the kitchen, finding a white linen tablecloth that looks like it's been freaking ironed, and a box of candlesticks, just as Seth said. I carry them outside, drape the tablecloth, and arrange the silver candlestick holders along the middle, adding three candles to each one. Devon has put napkins and wine glasses aside to go with the dinnerware, but I haven't the faintest clue how to make them they look pretty so it's a relief when he takes over.

Finally, after another half hour of hustle, everyone has gone, and I'm sipping a beer, waiting for Lena to get home. A car rolls up the drive, and I toss my beer in the trash and pop a mint before she makes it to the house. Straining my ears, I catch the faint sound of her voice as she says goodbye to Sydney, and then I hurry to the table to wait for her. The door opens, and she calls my name.

"Through here," I reply, and she appears like a vision in the doorway. The sexiest vision I've ever seen. She's wearing a wraparound silk dress that's new, and red pumps that strap halfway up her calf. I swallow my tongue. What's the bet she's also bought lingerie and is hiding it under that hot-as-fuck dress?

Her gaze follows the trail of petals all the way to the table, then lingers on the candles before landing on me.

Her brow furrows. "What's all this?"

I rise—because that seems like the kind of thing a gentleman would do at a time like this. "Did you have a nice day at the spa?"

"Best. Massage. Ever." She crosses to me and drops a kiss on my lips.

"Nuh-uh," I growl. "You're not getting away that easy." Wrapping my hand around the back of her neck, I sweep her legs out from under her and drag her onto my lap.

She wriggles her ass over my crotch. "You going to kiss me, or what?"

I give the lady what she wants, locking our lips, sweeping the inside of her mouth with my tongue. Tasting her, tasting my future. When she's nice and limp in my arms, I lift her onto the chair beside me. She makes an "oomph" and pouts. When I drop to my knees, her eyes fly open and the pout falls away.

"You want to know what I did while you were gone?" I ask her, holding her gaze and knowing I'll be happy to drown in her blue eyes forever. She nods, and slowly I raise my shirt. The surface of my skin burns, but I barely notice because Lena's attention is glued to me, and her throat bobbles as she swallows.

"Oh, my God," she whispers, shock written in her expression. "I can't believe you did that."

"Believe it, baby." I study her, trying to figure out whether she likes it. Based on the way her lips curve, I think she does, but my heart is in my throat as I drop my shirt and take her hands in mine. This is it. My big moment. More important than any championship fight. Scarier than any opponent I've ever faced.

I can't screw this up. I can't live without her.

"I love you, Lena LaFontaine, with everything I have and everything I am. I'm no poet, but you make me wish I was, so I could explain the way I feel. There are no words for it, at least, none that I know." Drawing in a deep breath, I release one of her hands and fish in my pocket until I find the little black box I collected earlier. "Since I can't tell you how I feel, the best I can do is show you. I want to dedicate the rest of my life to loving you." Opening the box, I offer the ring to her. "Marry me?"

"Oh, my God, yes!" She claims my mouth in a searing kiss, and then yanks at my collar. "Get off your knees, Jase."

I stand, grabbing her hand and slipping the ring on her finger. It looks right there. Like it belongs. Like she belongs to me. Damn right, she does.

"Do you like it?" I ask, wincing at the plea for reassurance in my voice.

Holding it up to the candlelight, she studies each facet, her smile growing broader and broader. Finally, she puts me out of my misery. "It's beautiful."

"Just like you."

"Jaaase," she groans, dragging a hand down her face. "So corny." Then she straightens. "Show me that tattoo again."

I strip off my upper half for her inspection. Her name is in bold letters across the center of my chest, a small silhouette of her face below.

"I really can't believe you did this," she says, although her smile is becoming smug. She likes having her name on me. Likes thinking of me as hers, for all the world to see. I get it, I'm the same. That's why her first tattoo was my name, on her ass. If I have my way, no one else will ever see it. But if they do... well, that motherfucker better think twice.

"I'd do anything for you," I murmur, extricating myself from her grip and pulling her to her feet, my hands linking at her lower back. "What do you think?"

"I think..." She nibbles on her lip, intentionally torturing me by drawing out her reply. "I think that I want every woman you ever meet to know you're mine, and this is a pretty straightforward way of doing it. Unsubtle. As your PR rep, I can't say it'll win you any female fans, but as your fiancé, I say it's freaking hot."

I pepper the length of her neck with kisses and soft bites, then sweep my tongue over it. She shivers in my arms.

"Want to show me how hot?"

"But what about dinner?" she asks.

Glancing at the covered dishes, waiting to be served, I shrug. "They can be reheated."

"Well, okay then." Sashaying away, she winks at me. "You're not the only one with a surprise tonight." She flicks her skirt up, giving me an eyeful of red silk garters on creamy white thighs. And is that a pair of crotchless panties...?

I chase after her, and she giggles and sprints into the house.

"Lena!"

Flashing those blue eyes over her shoulder, she asks, "Don't you mean 'future Mrs. Rawlins'?"

Oh, fuck. The words are so perfect, they nearly stop my heart. When I get my hands on her, she's not going to get away for a long, long time.

Like forever.

Maybe longer.

And she'll love every minute of it.

CPSIA information can be obtained
at www.ICGtesting.com
Printed in the USA
LVHW020541111122
732651LV00009B/768